# "Marry m

"Marry..." She shook her head in an effort to clear her mind. Surely Finn couldn't have spoken the words she thought she'd heard?

"Marry me and I promise you Edward will never recover from the shock."

Her smile was taut as she put down her glass, brushing his hand aside as if she had been unaware of it. "Now, Finn, it's getting late. And I think it's time to go, don't you?"

Alexandra Scott was born in Scotland and lived there until she met her husband, who was serving in the British army, and there followed twenty-five years of travel in the Far East and Western Europe. They then settled in North Yorkshire, and, encouraged—forcefully—by her husband, she began writing the first of some fifty romantic novels. Her other interests include gardening and embroidery, and she enjoys the company of her family.

## Books by Alexandra Scott

Don't miss any of our special offers. Write to us at the following address for information on our newest releases.

Harlequin Reader Service
U.S.: 3010 Walden Ave., P.O. Box 1325, Buffalo, NY 14269
Canadian: P.O. Box 609, Fort Erie, Ont. L2A 5X3

# HOLLOW VOWS
## Alexandra Scott

## *Harlequin Books*

TORONTO • NEW YORK • LONDON
AMSTERDAM • PARIS • SYDNEY • HAMBURG
STOCKHOLM • ATHENS • TOKYO • MILAN
MADRID • WARSAW • BUDAPEST • AUCKLAND

ISBN 0-373-17231-1

HOLLOW VOWS

Copyright © 1995 by Alexandra Scott.

First North American Publication 1995.

# CHAPTER ONE

BRIONY sat at the dressing-table in the familiar bedroom, but the face staring back at her might have belonged to a stranger despite all the familiar features. The wide, normally smiling mouth, the eyes Finn had once said mockingly she had imagined at the time were tawny, hypnotic and untamed as a tiger's... Finn Lawrence! Quite savagely, and in a futile effort to dispel his image, she bit at her lower lip, and a rather shaky hand was raised to touch the creamy skin, but there was no reassurance; nothing she could see or touch seemed to belong. Trembling, she reached out for the wine glass by her elbow and sipped, nose wrinkling as her tongue was offended by the warm, flat wine which had without doubt cost her father a small fortune...

Cream, she decided belatedly and with detachment, had never been her colour. A narrowed critical glance exaggerated its tendency to drain all life from her skin. It would have been so much more sensible to choose something less bridal, blue or green—black, she thought in sudden inspiration touched with hysteria, would in the circumstances have been entirely appropriate, but what did it matter after all...? With a despairing sobbing sigh she rose, smoothing the exquisite material over her feminine outline, out-spread fingers resting against her flat stomach. Nothing much in her life mattered from now on; it was——

'May I come in, darling?' Briony's head jerked up as her mother appeared in the doorway. She forced a smile. 'Are you decent?'

'Quite decent.'

'Briony!' The faintest touch of exasperation and amusement. 'I swear you've been sitting here dreaming and haven't even begun to change.' They were suddenly back in Briony's childhood as the girl was turned round, the mother dealing expertly with the row of tiny buttons which stretched from nape to waist. 'I knew you would never manage these on your own. You really ought to have let Julie help when she offered—it's part of the bridesmaid's duties after all...'

'I just wanted to have a little while to myself.' Surprised by a quite uncharacteristic urge to burst into tears, to wallow in her misery and to have her unhappiness dealt with by a comforting hug, some reassuring words, she sniffed, realising her mother was the very last person she could confide in...

'And here am I bursting in on you, robbing you of these last few moments before——'

'I didn't mean that,' Briony interrupted hastily before her mother could expound and maybe provoke actual tears. 'It's just...it's all been such a rush.'

'That's true,' her mother agreed with feeling, then, finished with the buttons, she stood with her arm about her daughter's waist, both of them facing the glass. 'Briony——' now it was she who was having difficulty with her emotions '—Daddy and I were so proud of you today.' Reaching up, she touched the wreath of flowers still circling her daughter's brown silky hair. 'You looked quite stunning. And we couldn't be more delighted that you've chosen Finn in the end and...' Turning away, she reached for the box of tissues and missed the look of stark dismay and desolation on her daughter's face.

So... it was right, then. What she had been afraid of, not a nightmare after all but bleak reality. No hope now of waking and discovering that all was well, that she was safely married to Edward Spurling whom she had loved all her adult life. Instead she had to recognise the truth: she had gone through a form of marriage with his cousin Finn Lawrence, a man whom she had never cared for... all to protect her stupid pride. *And*, she must be honest, to try to come to terms with her bitterness, to hit back at Edward who had so spectacularly betrayed her. All reasons which were now dust and ashes.

Just a month ago she had been happy. Not wildly euphoric because that wasn't her way. She had never been silly and gushing so had never yearned for anything more heady than the sense of steady content she found with the man she was going to marry. Happily she had set out for the party alone, because knowing she had a late duty it had seemed obvious and sensible that she should meet Edward there. After all, Duncan Harraby was *his* friend and they would have plenty to talk about.

It was crowded and noisy when she reached the top-floor flat. She had to force her way through the hall, searching faces as she pushed into the sitting-room, impatient after a week's separation to be with him again. But it was Finn Lawrence she caught sight of immediately, with that tiny *frisson* of irritability which characterised their meetings. In fact she was vaguely surprised to see him—it wasn't his scene, this slightly seedy bunch of entrepreneurs and City Hooray Henrys left over from the Eighties whom Edward racketed around with.

Finn was standing at the far side of the room beside an open French window, half a head taller than Edward, darker and...not more handsome, she wouldn't say that, just altogether more noticeable and that was why she had seen him rather than Edward who was to his left. Although, strangely, on this occasion the penetrating dark eyes, the ones that seemed to seek her out more often than she cared for, this time passed over her with no sign of recognition.

'Excuse me.' She thrust against the press of bodies, grinned and deftly extricated herself when Ben Pettigrew tried to sneak an arm about her waist, then, reaching the far side of the room, found her way firmly barred by a couple appar-

ently determined to solicit her advice on dealing
with a persistent back problem.

'Well, really, I would be glad to help if your
doctor should advise therapy and...'

'But you see...' After a moment Briony
switched off, sent an appealing glance over her
shoulder only to find that Edward and Finn were
involved in what appeared to be an intense discussion, not rowing exactly but certainly ex-
changing views with some force. So, what was
new? Finn had this habit of laying down the law
to Edward as if——

'So you see, Briony, if you could mention it
to Dr Wisley and...'

'What?' What *was* the woman talking about?
'Oh, that's not how the system operates.' She
edged a step backwards, leaning slightly to one
side so that her ear began to pick up some words
from behind.

'No, I'm damned if I will.' Finn was signalling
his usual impatience with his cousin. If only he
would be more tolerant, show some interest in
guiding the younger man who could, even she
was prepared to admit as much, be too impulsive
for his own good. Finn's next words were lost in
a burst of laughter close at hand and when he
spoke again it was noticeable that his voice, normally so warm, so full of mellow cadences, one
of the aspects of the man she could grudgingly
admire, today sounded harsh and abrasive.
'...refuse to do your dirty work for you.'

'Excuse me.' Abruptly, rudely she later supposed, she turned away from the Pattersons to find Edward with his back to her, knew he was still appealing to his cousin while Finn himself was regarding her morosely, almost with distaste.

'It would be easier coming from you, Finn.'

'Easier?' A shade of contempt now. 'Easier for whom?'

'Easier for——'

'Briony.' Whatever Edward had been about to say was stopped by Finn's intervention, speaking her name with pleasure and as if he had that instant caught sight of her. At the same time Edward jerked round, the easygoing features washed with red.

'Edward.' Difficult to explain the sudden certainty that she was in some way involved in their discussion, that her name was the one so deliberately cut off by Finn's recognition. A little chill wrapped about her heart. 'Darling.' She laced her fingers through Edward's, touched his cheek with hers. 'Having problems?' She did hope he wasn't in the process of changing his job again; it was so awkward making constant excuses to her parents who were by no means convinced that each move was an indication of his upward mobility.

'You could say that.' He avoided her eyes, stared down at their interlinked fingers, jumped guiltily when he was jostled on the other side and tried to detach himself from Briony.

'Hi.' A girl, someone Briony knew vaguely but whom she couldn't put a name to, was looking at her with considerable distaste. A short dark woman, pretty in a sharp way with sculptured black hair, black eyes and a thin, determined mouth, softened not a whit by a pale lipstick. Her hand, long fingernails painted to match her lips, rested on the sleeve of Edward's dark suit. There was something possessive about the gesture, a warning which caused Briony to raise an eyebrow, to simmer quietly with indignation. Just who did this...this woman think she was? She even glanced at Finn, inviting him to share her astonishment. But Finn was frowning in Edward's direction, with no time to spare for Briony's damaged ego.

'Darling.' The pink fingers curled still more protectively. 'Aren't you going to introduce us?' She smiled then at Briony, at least, rows of small white teeth showing briefly. 'Apparently not.' She extended her hand. 'I'm Pamela Price.' Their fingers barely touched. 'I'm Edward's fiancée.'

Briony felt the blood leave her head then—she was totally disorientated, bewildered and with an ache the size of a rock in her chest. If a chair had been handy she would have subsided into it, but as it was...

'Edward?' It was the faintest of queries but with the room spinning about her she couldn't summon the energy to be more decisive.

'Bri, don't make a fuss.' For the first time he looked directly at her, and she fancied tears were making the blue eyes even more brilliant than usual. 'Please!'

'Briony.' It was Finn's hand which came out to support her; she felt his strength and leaned gratefully against him. 'Why don't we leave this... this circus for the moment? It's not the place——'

'No.' Confidence raced back through her veins, and she thrust his arm aside. 'I would just love to know how it is that Edward——' if her voice grew sharp it was beyond her power to control it '—can have two fiancées. Is he planning to marry both of us or...?'

Not understanding how it happened, Briony found Finn had placed himself to one side of her and was skilfully manoeuvring her away from the obvious interest of fellow guests, out through the open French windows on to the terrace, and that Edward and the Pamela woman were following so for the moment there was some privacy.

'Now look here.' Finn sounded as grim as he looked. 'Unless you want everyone to hear every word, I suggest——'

'I don't care.' Briony couldn't quite control the tremor in her voice. 'I simply want to know what's going on. I've done nothing I need hide and——'

'And that, I suggest, is the more reason for you to show some restraint, Briony.' He was acting as if she were somehow at fault, disapproving, censorious. 'Whatever relief you might gain from bawling like a fishwife, you'd regret it in the morning.'

'I wasn't thinking of doing that,' she said as coldly as she could. 'And don't tell me, Finn Lawrence, what I'll regret in the morning.'

'Half that gaggle in there,' he went on as if she hadn't spoken, 'would give their eye-teeth to hear what's going on—the place is already buzzing. I'm going to suggest, why not go back to my flat? At least there——' he turned to glare at a couple who were about to step out on to the terrace and who abruptly changed their minds on encountering his icy look '—there you can be sure of some privacy.'

Briony gazed appealingly at Edward, whose attention was again elsewhere. It seemed to her there was everything to be said for Finn's suggestion, but Edward was reluctant to give even the slightest clue. Anyone would think he wanted to avoid a more intimate location... She glanced quickly at the other girl, who had for the past few minutes been eyeing her in that deliberately challenging way, but in the end it was Briony who looked away.

'Edward.' Mainly she was humiliated but at the same time she was blazingly angry as she reached out and gave his arm an impatient shake. 'For heaven's sake, why can't you say something? I don't see why it should all be left to your cousin; it's nothing to do with him, after all.' For a moment she glared at Finn as if it was his choice to be witness to her degradation, but when she encountered his sardonic look she quickly transferred her attention back to Edward. 'Do you want to go back to Finn's flat or don't you?'

'Might as well, I suppose.' He shrugged, making it clear the idea held little appeal for him. 'What do you say, Pammy?'

'If we must.' Clearly bored by the whole thing, she barely smothered a yawn. 'Not that I think it'll do any good.'

'Look.' Taking no trouble to conceal his impatience, Finn riffled in a pocket and produced a key, which he tossed in the air a couple of times then lightly in Edward's direction. 'As Briony said, it's really nothing to do with me but I'm telling you all, get out of here and solve your emotional problems in private. I know for a fact——' here he turned and stared pointedly at a man who was busy lighting a cigarette close to the terrace door, and waited until he took a step further away before continuing '—that at least two of our fellow guests supply gossip to the tabloid Press.'

'But——' Briony was puzzled '—who on earth would be inter——'

'Come off it, Briony.' Finn was curt to the point of rudeness. 'You must surely realise that the antics of Sir Julian Spurling's son are of paramount importance to the nation.'

'If you say so.' The coldness of her tone suggested some doubt; it was hard to imagine that simply because Edward's father had recently been knighted . . .

'Anyway, you know the way, Edward. Be my guests.' Finn was dismissive.

'Just a minute, Finn.' Edward caught his cousin's arm as he turned away. 'I thought you were coming too. I need you there.'

'Forgive me if I take a raincheck on this.' Finn's well-shaped mouth twisted in wry amusement. 'Sorting out your complex romantic troubles is no longer my scene, Edward.'

'No? Well, I just thought... Besides, I can take only the two of us in the Midget. I was hoping you might bring Bri——'

'Briony?' Finn's tone could hardly have been more reluctant and he appeared to be totally blind to the appeal in the striking eyes raised to his. 'Given the choice I'm pretty certain you would opt for a taxi—am I right?' There was a direct challenge and ... and something else she couldn't identify in the dark, intense look. At the same time it was impossible to avoid noticing how deeply fringed with lashes his eyes were, long and black and silky, the kind beautiful women would kill for. A shade or two darker even than the sable hair which fell over his forehead which he had a habit of brushing aside impatiently, as he was doing right now. And the impatience was evident in his voice too, the reaction of a busy man who didn't like his time to be wasted. 'Briony?' It was a second before she came back to the present and remembered exactly what was being discussed.

'Finn.' The thought of being on her own with the other two made her feel faint and Finn, whatever she might think, had always shown himself to be reliable. 'Finn, *please*. If you could, would do this last little thing for me.' She didn't even question such a strange choice of words, nor such a sudden desire for his support when previously it had been she and Edward against the world and especially against his cynical and highly critical cousin Finn Lawrence.

He stared down at her, disinclination in every line of the dark hawkish features, then his expression altered, eyes moved over her anguished appearance with something approaching sympathy. 'Well,' he shrugged, 'why not?' His mouth curled as if somewhere in this absurd fantasy he had found some diversion. 'But only——' putting an arm about her shoulders he propelled her in the direction of the French windows and the partying throng '—but only if you'll play a part for me. Gaze up into my face as if you find every word I utter so completely fascinating...'

Perhaps it was her expression of total disbelief, maybe even a flicker of the distaste which she felt but tried to conceal, maybe it was these which made the dark grey eyes widen in mocking appreciation, the white teeth gleam. 'While I— yes, I assure you I am being serious—while I tell you how utterly beautiful you look. And you must act as if you came here with one thought in your mind, to meet—maybe even to seduce— me. I can see——' he frowned comically as if they were in the throes of some light-hearted repartee

'—you'll have to call on all your acting skills, let your imagination run wild...'

'I'm afraid——' she spoke through gritted teeth '—even Dame Peggy Ashcroft would have rejected such a role as being much too far-fetched.' But even that cutting remark gave no indication of her distaste for the situation as they progressed through the room acknowledging one or two acquaintances and, while they lingered to exchange a few words, he had the arrogance to rest his cheek against her shining dark hair.

The tightness of his arm about her shoulders must have picked up her indignation and distaste but it thwarted her intention; they were stuck together as if fixed with Superglue, and it wasn't until the door of the flat closed firmly behind them that she was able to detach herself, glancing round briefly at Edward and his companion as the latter spoke.

'Quite a convincing display back there.' Searching in her handbag, finding her lighter, she applied the flame to the tip of her cigarette, her eyes narrowed as she drew the smoke deep into her lungs. 'I swear——' her laugh tinkled, and there was something entirely malicious about the way she subjected Briony to a slow and dismissive scrutiny '—half of Duncan's guests will be convinced that there was never anything between you and Edward...'

'Then they would be wrong, wouldn't they?' Briony's retort was instinctive but she regretted it when she heard the other woman's sharp ar-

tificial laugh again, saw the thin eyebrow scep-
tically raised. 'Anyway——' she felt compelled,
perhaps for Edward's sake more than anything
else, to justify herself '—it wasn't my idea. I
didn't see any need for that kind of play-acting.'
Now she glared accusingly at Finn.

'No?' His expression was all at once more
cynical, reminding her that after all it was she
who had sought his help. 'Well, maybe you ought
to reserve judgement on that until you hear what
cousin Edward has to offer by way of explanation.' Here he subjected the other man to a
look of quite withering dislike. 'If there is one.
Until then you have no idea what the needs of
the situation are.' The lift stopped and the four
stepped inside, Finn pressing the control button.
'But I agree with you, Briony, it wasn't a situation I found particularly pleasant, though you
must remember it wasn't one of my choosing.'

Damn him. Briony stood in the lift, the tip of
one shiny patent shoe tapping with impatience
and maybe a little nervousness, but it was very
useful to have him as a diversion. Without that
she would have been in danger of bursting into
tears, and she wouldn't want to give the Pamela
woman the satisfaction—she was quite smug
enough already. Without looking, Briony could
see the short fingers curled possessively round
Edward's arm, though—small satisfaction here—
Edward didn't look as if he was enjoying himself.
Serve him right.

A tiny shiver ran down her spine. She glared up at Finn, who had been studying her with rapt attention as he lounged in the corner of the lift. How dared he look at her with that raised eyebrow as if—colour flared in her skin at the very idea—as if she were one of the exotic species which he featured in his wildlife films...? The Curious Mating Habits of Late-Twentieth-Century Urban Female. Normally the idea would have been enough to cause her lips to curve upwards in appreciation, but certainly not when she was being treated like a subject at the end of a telephoto lens and also...

His last words finally registered and... Damn him, she thought again with more violence, why should it have been an unpleasant experience for Finn Lawrence? He wasn't involved emotionally and... In silence they crossed the car park.

'See you very shortly, then.' Finn dismissed Edward and his companion then held open the car door until Briony was seated, sweeping her long silky skirt inside before slamming the door shut. They were driving from the exit when she saw the lights of Edward's battered old sports car flick three times at the far end, his usual signal when they had arranged to meet somewhere. It brought the tears perilously close, so precluding any attempt at discussing the situation while they were driving. But by the time they pulled into the drive of the rambling brick house she had more or less got her emotions under control again.

She had never visited Finn's home before, nor had wanted to, but it wasn't at all what she would have imagined—*if* she had ever thought of it. TV producers lived in super modern flats, didn't they, filled with gleaming glass and chrome furniture? Either that or villas stuffed with Victorian bric-à-brac set off with Laura Ashley. But this was neither.

A large hall which might double as a dining-room—certainly there was a long table set about with dining chairs all in dull polished oak, the colour very nearly matching the wide strips of wood which formed the floor. At the far end under a massive lintel was an old brick fireplace where flames flickered brightly once Finn bent down and turned on a gas tap, and to the right a staircase led up presumably into the attic, since he had already explained he had had the large house converted and had chosen to live in the upper apartment.

'Through here.' He led the way into a comfortable sitting-room where two sofas covered in neutral linen stood either side of the fire. A wing armchair in bold terracotta with a book open on the floor beside it indicated where he usually chose to sit. She barely noticed the rather nice lamps brightening the corners; she was too compelled by the portrait over the mantel-piece. A fairly modern piece—the dress of the striking-looking woman told as much. Briony moved forward to look more closely.

'My mother,' he informed briefly, turning away to discourage any further discussion, and of course she understood that. She remembered vaguely hearing how his parents had been killed in some tragedy when Finn was more or less a schoolboy. 'If you'd like to give me your jacket...'

'What? Oh, all right.' But as she slipped her arms out of the sleeves, his fingers brushed against her skin, causing an automatic reaction which he misinterpreted.

'Are you cold, Briony?' This time his manner was less impatient.

'No, of course not.' But she was unable to control another tiny shiver, difficult to explain since the house was pleasantly warm. 'Not really,' she qualified, her smile wan.

'Shock, I imagine. Here.' He pulled a chair closer to the fire, removed and folded away a spark guard. 'I'll go and find you something to drink—what will it be? Tea, coffee? I can't recommend alcohol since——'

'Why don't they *come*?' She threw back her head and frowned, bit feverishly at her lip. 'Why is it that it takes Edward twice as long as... Can you tell me that, Finn?' Then she caught hold of herself. 'Sorry.' She tried to be casual, shrugged her shoulders. 'And why should you be put to so much trouble? You must be wishing you had never gone to that party. Come to think of it, Finn, it's not exactly the sort of place I'd have expected to find you, rather the reverse in fact.'

'Yes, well . . . we all behave irrationally from time to time. Now I'm going to put the kettle on.' She heard his feet crossing the hall and after a moment, unwilling to be alone with her thoughts and fears, she followed, standing in the doorway of the kitchen, watching as he took mugs from a cupboard and placed them on a tray. 'It's a lovely house, Finn.' She was struggling for normality, trying to act as if she had just dropped in for a casual visit because she found herself passing the door—not, she reminded herself with a bitter little stab, that any such behaviour would be normal where she and Finn were concerned. 'This kitchen——' her glance approved the central wood table, the expensive-looking oak cupboards which might have been there for a hundred years but most likely had not '—more like a farmhouse than a place near to central London.'

'Which is just what it was in the sixteenth century, though the land has long since gone under acres of concrete. I bought it as a wreck and spent a lot of time and even more money restoring it. I'd have liked to live in the country but it would be wildly impractical. This is a compromise. There are two acres of garden so it has a lot going for it. And I told you I've let the ground floor to a couple of students. That way, if ever I want to, the two flats can be turned into one again.' She watched him measure coffee into a jug, filling it with boiling water, placing it on the stove. 'So——' he was giving all his concentration to the thread of heat under the pot

'—tell me about yourself, Briony. I haven't seen you for nearly—what can it be, not far short of a year?'

'Mmm.' She was remembering how embarrassing that occasion had been, regretting that it had been brought up. 'About a year, I think. I'm still doing four days at St Barnaby's and I practise privately one day. Helps to pay the mortgage.'

'I've sometimes wondered if you were still there. It's just about ten minutes' walk from here as the crow flies, if that isn't too mixed a metaphor. Did you realise?'

'I thought it couldn't be far, but I wasn't paying that much attention when——' The doorbell rang just then, making her jump despite the fact that she had been waiting, every nerve and emotion quivering for that very sound, anxiety mounting to something very close to desperation. Now suddenly she felt very cold, clammy; the room began very slowly to revolve.

'Steady now.' Passing, he touched her arm briefly. 'You're going to be all right?'

She nodded, determined to ignore the sensation of nausea. 'Fine. It's just . . . I haven't had much to eat . . . You see, we . . . Edward and I, we always go for a meal after these affairs. It didn't seem to matter when I missed lunch, we were so busy in the department . . .'

'Well——' his smile was reassuring '—I do know all about missed meals, but look——' another blast from the door '—I must let them in.' He turned away. 'But if you want a minute, the bathroom is over there.'

But she was in the sitting-room, standing with her hands extended to the fire, swinging round with the appearance of composure when Finn led Edward and Pamela through.

Impossible to avoid comparing the two men, something she always tried to avoid since it so inevitably filled her with resentment on Edward's behalf. You'd almost think Finn had arranged for his cousin to be perpetually at a disadvantage. He wasn't that much smaller; you would hardly think a few inches would make so much difference. And although he was fairer, it was hard to say why that should be regarded as a handicap and——

'Briony.' There, she thought with irritation, he was being diffident, apologetic in a way Finn never would, no matter how wrong... And he seemed unable to look her straight in the eye.

'Well, I'll just go...'

That from Finn seemed to fill Edward with still more dire apprehension. 'But you promised——'

'... and get some coffee.' He paused by the door. 'Briony could do with a cup. I suggest we all could.'

'Not for me.' Pamela pulled a case from her bag, put a cigarette between her lips, touched a tiny flame to the tip and drew smoke impatiently into her lungs. 'But if you have anything stronger.'

'Help yourself.' Finn gestured towards an assortment of bottles and glasses on a half-moon table against a wall. 'I think you'll find something there, and if you feel the need of some ice just give me a call.'

'Edward.' When they were almost alone with Finn in the kitchen, Pamela clinking bottles and glasses, she took a step towards him, so close there was no longer any need for him to avoid looking at her, useless for him to pretend not to hear her whispered appeal. 'Edward, please.' Again his blue eyes were brilliant, brimming with barely concealed emotion, something which in spite of all her anxiety, all her irritation with him, she found deeply touching. But she couldn't blind herself to the air of relief with which he swung round to face Finn who at that moment came in with the tray, placing it on the small table between the two sofas.

'Briony——' he held out a mug, offered sugar and cream '—there are some biscuits in the tin and it might be an idea if we were all to sit down.' He chose one end of a settee, long legs stretched out in front, feet crossed at the ankle, Edward slumped down beside him. Briony had already sat on the edge of the seat opposite, but regretted it when Pamela declared in that hard, confident manner of hers how she preferred to stand since she had been sitting in the office for the largest part of the day and, in any event, they wouldn't be here for more than a few minutes. 'We do——' she ended her little statement with a meaningful glance at Edward '—have some important matters to attend to.'

Her crassness caused a wave of blind fury to envelop Briony. She put down her cup with a crash and sat forward in her seat. 'Edward!' If they had been alone she had the notion she might have put her hands on his shoulders and shaken him. 'I suppose——' simmering with anger she spoke through clenched teeth '—I suppose you are going to explain what this is all about.' Quite deliberately she refused to raise her eyes to the figure standing behind him, controlling him with those predatory fingers.

'I'm hating all this, you know that.' Now there was a note of accusation in his voice, as if the blame lay elsewhere; for a shocked instant she wondered if she were the focus. 'I'm no good at awkward situations, never have been...' Now a note of self-pity had crept in.

'What he is trying to say——' the sharp voice broke in.

'I was speaking to Edward.' Briony allowed her luminous eyes to rest for a second on the other woman before returning to the man she had planned to marry. 'Go on, Edward.' She was becoming exasperated and more impatient. 'But try to get to the point. And quickly please.'

'The fact is...' His whole attention was concentrated on his bone-white knuckles. 'I'm...' The pink fingers on his shoulder tightened. 'That is, Pam and I are going to be married.'

It was a moment before the mist cleared from her eyes. 'But...' The pain about her heart was more difficult. Vaguely she realised Finn had got up, had walked to the window where he stood for a moment staring out into the darkness before strolling back. But instead of returning to his original seat he perched close to Briony on the arm of the sofa, and although he was very nearly outside her line of vision, his nearness in some way gave her a little comfort even if that was by merest chance. Certainly she would never deceive herself that such a move had been planned to boost her confidence. She drew a deep breath. 'But that is impossible, Edward.' Her voice was more positive than she had feared it might be. 'You know perfectly well it is. I thought we——'

'Maybe you just made a mistake.' The brash voice suited her so well. 'It can be so easily done. It could be as simple as that.'

'Please, will you keep out of this!' Briony almost spat the words but her confidence was short-lived. 'Was it...was it that, Edward?'

'Look, I think we're getting all this out of proportion, don't you? Certainly it was never my intention to do anything to hurt either——'

'Edward!'

'So——' she ignored Pamela's interjection and now found the pain was easing just a bit '—if you really mean that, Edward, maybe it could be said I have a prior claim.' From behind she heard a disapproving mutter but right then her main concern was an ignoble desire to see that creature get her come-uppance.

'A prior claim?' There was amusement in the drawl, in the curl of the thin lips as the woman came round and joined Edward on the sofa, lying back, stretching as if she were wholly at ease. There was something close to triumphalism in the way she watched Briony, putting her cigarette to her mouth, drawing the smoke into her lungs, holding it while she leaned forward to tap ash into a dish. Then blowing it swiftly to one side, she raised her glass. 'You have a prior claim, sweetie——' there was no attempt to hide her malicious satisfaction '—only if you are more pregnant than I am. Shall we compare dates?' Another mocking salute with her glass before she drained it. 'Then we can race to the altar.'

A cold little draught coming from nowhere brought the sting of goose pimples to Briony's skin. There it was, then; the unacknowledged possibility which had been lurking on the periphery of her mind, which for most of the evening she had been forcing back. Now she stared at Edward, willing him to disclaim the story, urging him to laugh and shout April Fool or whatever, but he was avoiding her eyes, dared not look at her, so... This was how much she had meant to him... All the time she and Edward had been dating, planning, he and Pamela... She was feeling sick again, and faint; she glanced round at Finn who was still there, so close, watching her so sombrely. She had the absurd notion to reach out, to slip her hand into his, to borrow a little bit of strength from him and... It was an effort to face the other two; that showed in her voice, weak, disembodied. 'Oh.' Swallowing did nothing to dislodge the lump in her chest. 'Oh, I see.' She sensed rather than saw that Finn had leaned forward, his arm extended along the cushions at her back.

'From that I gather you're no longer prepared to argue?' Triumph and maybe a shade of relief.

'No.' She put a hand to her head, wondering why it felt as if it had been packed with cotton wool. 'At least not on your terms.'

'Well, shall we go, Edward? Now that it has all been cleared up, there seems no point...'

Obediently he rose, put out a hand towards her, looked hurt when she jerked her head away to avoid any contact. She would have hated him to know how hard she had to struggle against her instinct to capture his hand to hold it against her cheek in a final desperate attempt to keep him. And maybe it was Finn's arm coming round her shoulders which gave her the determination to hang on to her pride; certainly she had no inclination to reject *his* consoling gesture...

'And I hope by this time even you know——' his blatant anger too was a help, perhaps keeping her from making a complete fool of herself '—what a damnable mess you've made of things.'

'Look, Finn, you've told me as much already and don't think I don't know. This is one of the crass situations which I never imagined I'd find myself in. But it's not altogether my fault . . . At least . . .'

This time Briony could not entirely blame Pamela for seizing him by the arm. 'Let's go,' was hissed through clenched teeth, and Edward seemed to offer little resistance as he was hurried towards the hall. She was still standing in the same spot when the outer door closed. Firm footsteps sounded on the wood floor, then, sensing his nearness, she turned and gave Finn one swift glance before she was staring down at her fingers, twisting her handkerchief into knots and fighting back the tears.

'I wish you had told me, Finn.' Her voice was not entirely steady as she slid weakly back on to the sofa. 'If you had, then I'd have been pre-pared, might not have made such a total fool of myself.'

'You didn't ask.' The shrug was something she sensed rather than saw. 'And when did you ever believe anything I might have to say about Edward?'

Remembering their last meeting, she could do nothing other than shake her head, a single swift move which had her hair floating out from her skull, its gleaming silky length picking up the flicker of flames from the fire and seeming to hold Finn's attention in endless thrall. Then he sighed, shrugged.

'Besides, you didn't. Make a fool of yourself, I mean.'

But her mind was still on his earlier accusation, one which she could hardly deny. 'You're quite right. I probably wouldn't have believed you. Besides, why should you do Edward's dirty work for him? You've been doing that forever, and there comes a time...' Not thinking what she was doing, she reached out for a cushion, shook it out and, rather to her surprise, she managed to get to her feet. She even produced a faint smile, wan and painful to see. 'Finn, if you could ring for a taxi—you must be dying to have your flat to yourself again; it's been the most awful imposition...'

'No need for that.' Going into the hall, he returned with her jacket, slipped it around her shoulders. 'You're still in Hallows Terrace?'

'Yes. How did you know that?' Moving towards the door like an automaton, she remembered her handbag beside the sofa and turned back abruptly, bending down to pick it up, and that was when things began to get really rough. As she straightened up she found the room was moving, slowly at first then with gathering speed. Finn was on the ceiling and then on the floor and she had no idea where she was, except that for an endless moment the laws of gravity, the rules of nature, went haywire. It was horrid and frightening, so that when the darkness came it was very nearly a relief.

'Shh. Shh, Briony.' The sounds of her own weeping and coughing, disgustingly wet and humiliating, brought her back to the present, to where she was half sitting, half lying on the sofa, legs stretched out, piles of cushions at her back and Finn comforting her in the most practical way possible, by putting a box of tissues close to her hand and an arm about her shoulder till the paroxysm eased. 'You scared me half to death.' He spoke with comforting accusation and a trace of amusement. 'You know that?'

'Sorry.' A weary smile. 'Did I pass out?'

'Completely.' His grin couldn't entirely hide his concern. 'Luckily the settee was handy and I was able to reach you in time to slide you on to it.'

'Oh, Finn.' She bit her lip in a feverish and completely useless attempt to keep the tears at bay.

'I know, I know.' Sounding the least little bit impatient, he got up, stood, hands thrust into the pockets of his trousers, very nearly enjoying a situation he could treat with world-weary cynicism. 'You're feeling miserable, wallowing in your misery, and it's much too early for me to tell you that given time you'll recognise a lucky escape if ever there was one. And since I can't mention that, you did say something about having missed out on lunch and that makes two of us, so why don't I take you out for a meal? Food, I've always believed, is quite the best cure for a broken heart, and even a slightly scratched one has been known to benefit from a plateful of Giuseppe's famous *osso buco*. It's only about ten minutes' stroll if you think you can make it.'

'I couldn't eat a thing.' How could anyone be so crass, just mentioning food in the face of her anguish? And he positively enjoyed that little joke about a scratch, though she might have known what his attitude would be; he had always had a very jaundiced view of her relationship with his cousin.

Every word he spoke about the *osso buco* was true, she found, especially when washed down by a particularly delicious Barbaresco which Giuseppe assured them was produced in the valley in Piemonte where he grew up.

'That was delicious.' When she had caught the last drops of delicious liquor on a hunk of bread and eaten it, she wiped her mouth with the napkin. 'Thank you, Finn.'

'I'm glad.' He was entirely straight-faced. 'At least your appetite is intact.' She even began to smile then, but recollection returned, driving out any inclination to amusement.

'I suppose...' The striking amber eyes seemed to darken though the candle on the table reflected the odd glimmer. 'I suppose——' her long capable fingers crumbled a piece of dry bread, '—maybe it was all my fault... At least——'

'For God's sake, Briony, don't be such a fool.' His sudden irritability was contained only by the arrival of Giuseppe, who began to whisk their plates away while accepting their compliments on the dish, and Briony found time to sympathise with Finn. He must be sick to death of having to cope with the aftermath of his cousin's emotional problems. He was still frowning when they were again left alone. 'Edward's getting his boss's daughter pregnant can hardly be laid at your door.'

'His boss's daughter?' That was what had slipped her mind, what she had forgotten in all the long drama of the evening. 'Of course.' Maybe there was even some comfort to be found in the information. 'Of course, that would make it so much more difficult for him.' Gnawing at her lip, she drove away the tears. 'Wouldn't it?' she appealed.

'Make it very convenient for him, I'd say.' Always a harsh critic, always with his knife in. 'One of the tried and tested ways to progress in your career is to marry the boss's daughter; it's pretty near infallible.'

'How can you say——!'

'Easily I can say it. Edward is nearly twenty-seven years old, as clear a case of arrested development and over-indulgence as I've come across. And as for its being your fault, there was no obligation for him to impregnate the girl.' Briony closed her eyes to the picture he was trying to force on her—she didn't want to imagine but certain images would not be obliterated. 'I don't for a moment suppose she forced him. And look at it this way——' his manner compelled attention no matter how mutinous she felt, but still there was no need for him to be so graphic about it; he must realise how wounded she felt and . . .

'—so far as we know, Pamela had no commitments. *He* did. He had a firm commitment to you, Briony, at least...' His eyes were speculative and for a moment she didn't understand, then...

'Are you doubting me?' It seemed the final betrayal.

'What I'm saying——' leaning across, he covered her hand with his '—is that I swear I never heard from Edward that wedding bells were ringing for the pair of you.'

'Well, you hardly ever see him—you're always abroad, aren't you? And anyway——' crazy in the circumstances that she should be putting forward a word in Edward's defence '—you've never troubled to hide the fact that you dislike him.'

'Point number one.' His hand was withdrawn and he played with the stem of his glass. 'I've seen him often enough in the past few months for him to have given me a clue that your relationship was serious. Point number two: I don't dislike him but I do know him, and I can tell you he's not for you. If you remember, I said as much to you some time ago.'

'That was just pique.' Forced against her will to recall the occasion, she flared out at him. 'I'm sure you're not used to having your invitations refused. You're the great Finn Lawrence, famous TV personality and womaniser—you didn't like it when I said I couldn't go out with you because I had a date with——'

'Yes.' He was amused more than put out by her attack. 'You're right, it was a novel experience. I did think it strange that you should prefer—what was it?—a trip to the local disco rather than the world première of a first-rate film.'

'Well, at least I was glad you didn't pine. I saw your picture in the paper with Valentina Barossa—she made a far more suitable, much more glamorous companion for you than I ever would.' Eyes flashed across the table while she waited for him to deny that comparison, but of course she had always known Finn Lawrence was the most perverse, the most maddening man in the world and... 'Anyway, it wasn't a disco, it was a twenty-first birthday party.' One of Edward's friends, she reminded herself, a party she had not enjoyed, and even at the time she had had a tiny sense of regret that she had made a bad decision.

He shrugged, his amusement evaporating quickly. 'I think I remember telling you at the time, suggesting that you were throwing yourself away on Edward. In spite of all appearances to the contrary, the family isn't nearly as affluent as outsiders might imagine.'

'So...' She frowned, for the moment confused, unable to grasp his meaning, then when she did her first inclination was to laugh, the implication was so fanciful. 'Oh, dear, is that what you really think of me, Finn?' Momentarily it gave her pleasure to tease, but his face was impassive. 'I promise you——' she leaned closer '—I'm not intending to marry Edward because I thought, however mistakenly,' she mocked, 'that he was rich. I'm not really a gold-digger. But on the other hand——' she frowned, losing her taste for the game '—I can't imagine why you should be so spiteful about them... I understood that—didn't they bring you up after your...?' Looking up into his face, she was quite suddenly frozen by the expression. 'I mean...' she stammered, 'no one would believe ... Didn't your uncle get his knighthood because of all the money he gives to charity?'

'Let's forget about Sir Julian.' It was noticeable that he avoided the relationship. 'We were talking about Edward rather than his father. All I'm saying, Briony, is I'd hate to see a woman like you making a mistake, finding herself tied for life to a much weaker man.'

'And who would you like to see me tied to then?' Anger, irritation spilled out then. All she had hoped for over recent years, all she had worked for was being cheapened by his attack on Edward, who was no longer here and able to defend himself. 'Someone macho and dominant, I suppose, someone with an image and a flashy lifestyle.' The words spilled from her lips without consideration. 'In short, someone more like Finn Lawrence.' She stopped abruptly then, aghast at the words she had spoken, words which she knew had never entered into any waking thought.

'Now——' it was a long time before he spoke and when he did he was calm, reflective, considering in a way she knew she did not deserve '—now there's a thought.'

'Oh, God, Finn, I'm sorry. So sorry.' Shame washed over her in engulfing waves; she could hardly raise her head to look into his face but forced herself. 'I don't know why I'm acting like this, getting at you when none of it is your doing. It's Edward's fault and——'

'And not yours as you claimed a minute ago?' At least he didn't seem angry or contemptuous, as he had every right to be.

'Maybe.' She shrugged. 'At least . . . I'm sure Edward would try to persuade everyone . . .' Her voice shook. She bit her lip, unable to explain even to herself why she was bothering with explanations, especially to Finn Lawrence, the last person she would normally have chosen as a confidant; and yet there was a compulsion . . . 'You see——' a forced little smile '—Edward always did say I was a throwback, behind the times.' An inhibited Victorian miss was the epithet he had once tossed at her in a mood of frustration. 'I suppose——' faint colour stained her cheeks as she went on '—I suppose what it boils down to is that *she*——' the venom in her tone startled her '—was more accommodating than I was.'

Without looking at him she was conscious of his scrutiny; doubtless, her imagination taunted, doubtless he was regarding her with all the interest one reserved for a species previously thought to be extinct. She felt the warmth in her cheeks, jerked her head up when he finally spoke. 'Well, at least that seems to relieve us of one worry.' Her raised eyebrow and uncomprehending look brought an explanation. 'Remember, Pamela did challenge you on that point.'

'I'm not pregnant.' Her voice was as scathing as she could make it; she was wounded that he should even be thinking along the same lines. 'But of course I realise you have only my word for that.'

She thought she heard him sigh before he spoke again, and when he did his voice was gentle.

'And doesn't it occur to you, Briony, that if Edward had really been in love with you neither Pamela nor anyone else would have been acceptable as a...stand-in.'

'Of course he loves me.' The words burst passionately from her lips. She was stunned that he could keep turning the knife in her wounds— he might have been enjoying himself but she was not prepared to have the last remnants of her pride stamped into the dust. 'He almost said that, didn't he? You must have heard him.' A sob was hastily swallowed. 'He's as desolate as I am; every word he said told me that, told us all...'

'Edward always did, always will say what is most appropriate to the occasion, Briony. If it made life easier for him to imply desperate regret, then that is what he would do. But...I can see you don't like my interpretation, only...since you brought the subject up maybe you could answer another question: did you find it all that easy to hold him off, assuming of course that you are, as you say, so desperately in love with him?'

'I *am* in love with him.' She spoke with icy anger.

'Ah——' he smiled then, knowingly, sympathetically, making her long quite irrationally to lash out at him '—but did you love him so desperately that your resistance was forever on the point of crumbling, so much that when he begged, pleaded, you were having to hang on to your virtue by the skin of your teeth, that you were always on the brink of being swept away with your own emotions? Sorry to mix so many metaphors, but were you so longing to cast discretion to the winds, to——?'

'I'm not going to discuss my feelings; especially I'm not going to discuss them with you, Finn Lawrence. Why is it that so many men think of nothing—nothing,' she repeated on a rising note, 'but sex at its most basic?'

He laughed then, very softly, as if in her innocence she had told him everything he had ever wanted to know about her relationship with Edward. Certainly she herself had never felt less like laughing. 'Now,' she invited coldly, 'it's getting late, I've had a ghastly day, so if you do mean to take me home rather than keep me all night——'

'Another inviting prospect.' Then before her anger had time to flare, 'Tell me, Briony, just what are your feelings for Edward right now?'

'A woman scorned? Is that what you're thinking? Well, right.' The golden eyes sparkled contempt at his curiosity but there seemed little point in concealment at this stage. 'I have all the feelings you might expect: I feel bitter, angry, furious, disgusted.' She hesitated, but the admission was already spilling from her lips. 'I feel humiliated and——' her voice had begun to shake so she caught her lower lip between her teeth and stood like that for a few minutes until she had regained control '—and so degraded I don't know how I'm going to deal with it.'

'Good!' His whole-hearted approval was for a moment surprising, even shocking. 'Good,' he repeated, clenching his right hand and thumping it into his left open palm. 'Then hit back, for heaven's sake. And hit hard. That's the only way to cope with the feelings you're describing.'

'Wouldn't I love to!' His reaction was almost a diversion; she gave a faint smile and shrugged her shoulders. 'If I could think of a way, an effective way, I would grab the opportunity with both hands.'

'Would you, now?' There was intense speculation on his face; the eyes, dark and shadowy, were concentrating on her mouth; she was very nearly compelled to run the tip of her tongue over her lips and... 'If I were to suggest a way, a way which would entirely reverse the situation, which would be the last thing Edward would be expecting, what, I wonder, would you say?' Her wide-eyed attention denoted interest, the soft lips parted as the excitement of such a possibility fired her imagination. 'A response,' he continued persuasively, 'which would hit Edward and——' he was watching her closely as a panther might a gazelle '—yes, maybe even Pamela, with all the devastating power of an Exocet missile.'

'I'm listening.' Her manner was abstracted, for she was more than listening, she was rejoicing in the opportunity he appeared to be holding out to her. If only she could hit back at . . . at both of them, if she could return to them just a little of the hurt and disillusion they had caused. 'Go on, Finn.'

It was late, and but for the soft strains of some Neapolitan love song it was quiet in the restaurant. The other diners, apart from a preoccupied couple at the far end, had gone; Giuseppe was polishing glasses behind the bar in the opposite corner. She leaned forward, one hand going out to touch the stem of her wine glass, the other lying on the pink and white tablecloth. 'Go on,' she said again, this time in a voice that was breathy with anticipation. And her mind was cloudy so that for a moment she failed to absorb the significance of the words.

'Marry me, Briony.' His hand came out to cover hers, his thumb moving idly over her wrist, stroking the fine hairs, causing havoc to her senses. 'Marry me and I promise you Edward will never recover from the shock.'

'Marry . . . ?' She shook her head in an effort to clear her mind. Surely he couldn't have spoken

the words she thought she had heard, but
somehow the intensity of his manner, his air of
watchfulness convinced her, and she knew a
moment of quite crushing disappointment. For
the second time in a few hours she had been
cruelly misled. How could she have been so
foolish as to trust him, and how could she
possibly extricate herself and salvage a few shreds
of her dignity? Her smile was taut as she put
down her glass, brushing his hand aside as if she
had been unaware of it, and got to her feet. 'Now,
Finn, we both know you're being utterly ridiculous. It's getting late——' a swift glance at her
watch '—and I think it's time to go, don't you?'

# CHAPTER TWO

'How could you, Finn?' During the trip from the reception, Finn's attempts at conversation were largely unsuccessful, dwindling to silence, but the moment the hotel door closed behind them the dammed-up frustration burst from her. Until that instant she had been moving in a dream, disembodied almost, looking down on the day's events as if from above, seeing this ridiculously handsome privileged couple: Briony Maxwell—no, she corrected herself with a tiny shiver of apprehension, Lawrence now, in law at least—in velvet skirt and waistcoat just a few shades darker than her eyes, a blouse in toning jewel colours; Finn in a dark suit, white shirt, distinguished claret tie, as devastating as she had ever seen him, dark hair falling over his forehead, pink rose in his buttonhole—oh, yes, all the appurtenances of the fashionable wedding scene— white teeth gleaming with appreciation at one of the usual risqué jokes.

Then the fine eyes turning to watch as the bride slowly descended the staircase, pausing at the half-landing to throw the bouquet in the direction of the excited gaggle of younger female guests. There was deliberation in the way she just avoided looking directly at him; that telephone call as she was passing her parents' bedroom had turned her heart, already in cold storage, into permafrost. But the smile was still firmly fixed; for the sake of her parents the act had to go on, certainly not for the sake of the stranger she had married with almost indecent haste.

But she couldn't, no matter what her inclination, wipe away the expression of pride and pleasure her mother was now showing. It had been so hectic for them dealing with all the details which the high-profile wedding they wanted for their only child demanded.

'Nonsense, my pet.' Her father had brushed aside her protest as if it were a foolish whim. 'We simply won't hear of a quiet wedding. Your mother and I have been planning this for ten years and nothing you can say is going to do us out of it. Besides, Finn is a well-known personality. I'm determined to show him off, make all our friends wildly jealous,' he teased.

And at the time, still slightly traumatised by the speed with which it had all happened, she had lacked the energy to argue. It was only now, when the bedroom door had closed on her and her new husband, that she began to return to reality.

'How could you?' Again she threw the question, then before he could answer she whirled away, stood looking out of the window, oblivious of the coming and going of traffic far below, barely noticing the huge jet climbing high after taking off from Heathrow.

'If you would explain what you're talking about.' His voice was cagy; without even turning she knew exactly how he'd be looking at her, that narrowed speculative expression indicating he had some idea of her meaning.

'Please don't prevaricate.' Voice not quite steady, she swung round to confront him, but her arms moved protectively about herself, hands rubbing against the silk of her blouse as if even in this overheated room she were feeling shivery. 'You know perfectly well what I mean. I spoke to Edward just before we left home.'

'Ah.' One dark eyebrow arched in what she interpreted as cynical comment. 'I wondered if that was it. So——' his expression grew more sombre '—tell me, Briony, what exactly are you trying to say?'

'I should think it was obvious, for heaven's sake.' She just managed to restrain her inclination to spit the words at him. 'I'm saying, asking, why you didn't say Edward had been trying to contact me?'

'Would you believe——?' He surveyed her resentful face for a moment then went on. 'No, I can see you wouldn't, but the truth of the matter is I had no intention of allowing you to be upset when——'

'Upset?' In crescendo she cut him off. 'Why should I be upset when Edward told me...?' She came to a halt, biting at her lower lip as she tried to regain her self-control.

'When he told you...what?' The icy calm was making all kinds of insinuations about her character, then as she didn't respond he smiled bitterly. 'Could it be that Edward told you he was having second thoughts about his marriage to Pamela?'

'Well, I was entitled to be told.' Aware of handling this difficult situation so ineptly did little for her composure. She felt colour coming and going in her cheeks as he continued to look down at her.

'As to that, you've just told me that is exactly what Edward did say; you heard it from the horse's mouth, so to speak.'

'But don't you see——?' A touch of hysteria; she recognised the shrillness, tried to be calm, more reasoned. '*After* the wedding, when it was too late.'

He was carved in stone, so still she hardly expected him to speak again, then his lips moved; the words, so soft, almost casual, were yet caustic with contempt. 'You're telling me——' he could hardly believe it '—you are saying...you still harbour feelings for the man. After what has happened, you'd still be prepared to forgive, to have him back. *Is* that what you're saying?' His manner demanded a denial she could not offer.

'All I'm saying is I had a *right* to know, damn it.'

'A right to know.' Suddenly she felt herself menaced as his iron control seemed about to loosen. He strode towards her with such an air of fury that it took all her will to stand her ground without flinching. 'All right then, you have a *right* to know so I'll tell you, shall I? And don't——' his lips were tight against his teeth as he spoke '—don't ever accuse me of spilling the beans. I truly meant it——' a brief humourless laugh '—yes, I meant it when I said I was trying to protect you. You see, Cousin Edward rang me two days ago. I had already warned him against accepting his wedding invitation—he had made some vague arrangement about his new job with Price's, taking off to some seminar. But he rang to tell me Pamela had gone into a nursing home with a threatened miscarriage.'

'Ah.' The noise in her ears, like gushing water, stopped up her mind, affected her balance so that she was forced to reach out one hand for the back of a chair, her eyes closed to shut out the pain, the long dark lashes lying like tiny fans against the creamy skin. Thus it was that she missed the look of concern on Finn's face, sensed his nearness only when her nostrils picked up the evocative spicy scent of his cologne. She opened her eyes. The hand she raised was instinctive, something he could not know and which was all too easily judged as a rejection. His eyes narrowed again.

'Ah...so I was right. You didn't know.'

Pressing her lips firmly together, she shook her head. It was a moment before she could find some words. 'Not that it was particularly relevant.' The ache in her chest was telling an entirely different tale.

It was an age before he spoke and the words were preceded by a short scoffing laugh. 'No?' A sigh as he turned, walked to where their cases were stacked at the foot of the bed. 'I would have said that was exactly what it was—*particularly* relevant.'

His coldness, the suggestion of scorn, faint though it was, made her simmer with anger. Lips pressed tightly together, she watched him unzip his case and throw it open, felt her emotions change, coalesce, as she saw a very expensive pair of silk pyjamas being tossed on to the bedcover. In the turmoil of recent weeks the basic facts of their situation had been pushed to the back of her mind—it was something she had been meaning to speak about but for one reason or another the time had never been right. Only now was it right back in force, hammering for attention although . . . the middle of a rather acrimonious discussion was hardly the best time to bring up the subject of their intimate relationship. If only he had been at home a bit more, not rushing about so much, being so elusive . . . Panic fuelled by more than a touch of self-pity mounted . . . 'Well——' she only just managed to stop herself shouting out the words '—there's no point in going into that again, but I just think it was unfair of you to keep it from me.'

'Look, Briony——' the gleam in his eyes was a sudden reminder of an explosion of temper she had witnessed once or twice in the past; she had the impression he too was struggling for control '—I've grown weary of carrying the can for Edward and as sure as hell I'm not going to have him muscling in on our honeymoon.'

'Wh...?' His words were less than reassuring, though in view of her own recent thoughts scarcely surprising. 'What do you mean? I thought...' Confused by his cynically raised eyebrow, she lost her thread. 'I didn't think...'

'Go on,' he invited sarcastically, making it clear he was toying with her, enjoying her discomfiture. 'You thought...or you didn't think...what?'

'Will you stop this?' A sob broke from her; a hand went up to cover her eyes as she fought her weak emotions. 'Finn, for heaven's sake, it's not as if we...as if we married for the usual reasons.'

'Tell me what you mean, Briony.'

'You must know what I mean, but since you insist... You spoke of a honeymoon. Even you must agree that is... well, for lovers.'

'And you, I presume, don't see us in that role?' As he spoke he sighed in mocking dejection and strolled round the bed towards her, throwing off his jacket and pulling at his tie. 'You're not answering,' he challenged, making no concessions to her obvious misery. 'And yet, I swear, all our friends at the wedding imagined that is exactly what we are. You played your part with

such enthusiasm I was in danger of being carried
away with the idea myself.'

'Finn.' She couldn't imagine why she was appealing to his good nature. 'You know I had no
choice. I had to play the part as well as I could
for my parents...'

'Ah, yes,' he agreed, nodding as if in full
accord. 'And they were as convinced as anyone
else. As I said, a masterly performance.' Though
he was still lightly mocking, she was disturbed
by his air of bleakness.

'Anyway, you knew the score; the whole idea
was yours and no one else's...'

'And why did you think I made the suggestion
in the first place, Briony?'

'Don't you think I haven't asked myself that
question a hundred times?' Again on the brink
of tears, she brushed past him, striding over to
the window, looking out, then turning to face him
challengingly. 'A hundred times I've asked myself
what you'd be getting out of the deal.'

'Well, now——' swinging round a pink satin
chair, he sat astride it, arms resting on the back.
'—I did have the notion that I'd be getting myself
a wife. That I understood to be the bargain.'

'Oh, no.' Watching him cagily, she shook her
head, felt her hair billow silkily out from her
head. 'Oh, no—what you wanted, Finn
Lawrence, was to get back at Edward; you've
always been jealous of him.' Even as she chose
the words she regretted them, knew she would
have them thrown back into her face.

'Jealous?' It was a surprise to find she had caught him on the raw. 'Why in heaven's name should I be jealous of Edward?'

'I don't know why, I just know you've always given that impression. And I think you saw the perfect means of paying him back.'

'I rather thought——' rising quickly, he came towards her and, when she refused to look at him, put a finger beneath her chin so that she was forced '—I rather thought the idea was for you to pay him back, my sweet. You, after all, were the one who went completely to pieces when Pamela sprang her little surprise that night.'

'But now——' she wanted to put her hands over her ears and refuse to listen; besides, his words were a reminder of what might have been '—but now it looks as if she's out of the picture.'

'And you? You are imagining you're right back in the frame, is that it? You and Edward could have put it all behind you and lived happily ever after—that's what you're thinking?'

'What if it is?' She refused to be other than defiant.

'I'd be surprised if any woman could ever live happily with Edward, although of course I may be biased. But apart from that ignoble comment, do you really think that Edward, enjoying for the first time in his life some of the trappings of success—the company car, the name on a brass plate on his office door—do you really think he'd be prepared to jeopardise all that so he could marry you? Whether or not Pamela is still pregnant?'

'These things don't matter to Edward,' she protested hotly, though entirely without conviction. 'He has never been even slightly ambitious.'

'You do defend him, don't you?' His voice grew perceptibly harder. 'Wouldn't you say there's something distasteful about a woman speaking up for a man who has behaved as badly as Edward has? It has an unpleasant whiff of masochism about it.'

'How dare you imply...?' Feverishly she bit her lip. 'Anyway, you've always known how I felt about Edward.'

'Yes.' He sighed. 'That's quite true, I've always known how you felt about Edward. I could never understand it, but there...' Watching, she saw him pick up the pyjamas, ram them down in the case. 'Life is full of disappointments, only——' the case was closed with a vicious little tug '—if your feelings were so intense, why didn't you fight for him? Why didn't you insist he keep his word and marry you... if as you say that was *his* inclination as well?' His manner implied a question could be raised on that last point.

'Of course it was what he wanted, you *know* that.'

'Then, as I say, it seems strange that you simply lay down and let the pair of them walk all over you. If you had put up more of a fight, who knows?' He smiled coldly, cynically. 'It might have been Edward who was sharing this room with you and that——' he lifted his case and turned towards the door '—that would have been unalloyed joy for you both. Or else——' his hand reached up for the doorknob '—an unmitigated disaster.'

'What . . . ?' That last dig scarcely registered. 'Where are you going?'

He grinned, shrugged philosophically. 'Well, since you have made it so clear that you're still dazzled by Cousin Edward and since I don't rate my self-control that highly and since——' he sighed deeply as if the list of provisos was almost too much '—since I don't want you to be lying there in all your virginal finery trying to turn me into Edward, I think it would be best for me to find myself another bed, don't you?'

Relief. She was almost certain that was what she was feeling; whatever it was, it flooded through her. 'But...won't they think it strange?'

'Undoubtedly. But right now their reactions don't interest me that much. Anyway, it's been a long day, Briony. If I were you I'd get into bed, and if you want anything to eat you can always call room service. And...I'll see you at breakfast, OK?'

The door closed, she staring in disbelief, uncertain whether she wanted to laugh or cry. It had been so incredibly easy—if she had planned it all down to the final detail it could not have gone more smoothly; so easy in fact that it was difficult to reconcile with her own self-image, for...she had always had this deep-down belief that Finn rather fancied her.

Well, now—she determined to be fair—not fancied exactly, but she had cherished the idea that he liked her, that given the chance he'd be more than happy to share a bed with her; but wasn't that true of any man you were likely to meet? Their main preoccupation seemed concerned with persuading one girl or another to slip beneath the sheets with them, and yet here was Finn Lawrence, who had gone to the extremes of marriage and...and who was apparently content to walk away from what was perfectly legal.

So it was all a delusion that Finn had liked her quite a lot, and now she was left on her own nursing a sense of anti-climax, the very last thing—colour washed her cheeks—the last thing you would expect, especially when the wedding had in the end turned out to be quite a romantic affair.

But no, she resolutely refused to go along that route; instead she began to drag off her clothes, throwing them with abandon on to a chair before she headed for the shower. After that, she promised herself, she was going to take his advice. She was pretty certain she would be asleep as soon as her head touched the pillow; it had been an exhausting day at the end of an exhausting few weeks and...

And this nightdress, the one so conveniently at hand when she opened the case, the one her mother with all sorts of romantic sighs had bought, could hardly have shouted honeymoon any louder. A scrap of lace for the top, narrow straps and a slinky skirt in champagne satin which slithered seductively against her skin. It was heaven to wear, she found, and she couldn't find the energy to search in her case for something more discreet.

Minutes later she had brushed out her hair, cleaned her teeth and was emerging from the bathroom, hand on the light cord, when the door from the corridor was suddenly thrown open. Her eyes widened in alarm until she realised exactly who was there. Finn—he had come back. Her heart began to thump against her ribs, one hand moved to her throat in a vain attempt at modesty, and at the same time she experienced a feeling not far short of joy that she was wearing the most luxuriously seductive garment she had ever possessed.

He was motionless, leaning against the closed door, and no matter how casual his manner there was no doubting the intense awareness of the gleaming eyes nor the way they were taking in every detail of her appearance. For what seemed an eternity they stood facing each other until at last he spoke.

'Sorry if I startled you, Briony.' It was a shock for her to discover that, far from feeling threatened, she was actually stimulated, excited by the unexpected encounter, was looking forward to his next move, was holding her breath as he levered himself upright and took a step in her direction. 'I just remembered I had left my shaving things in the bathroom.' In spite of its low timbre his voice, she noticed for the first time, had a hard edge, and in this context how easy it was to come to the conclusion that it was a cynical acknowledgment of feminine artfulness, that in some perverse way she had expected him to come back and dressed accordingly.

So when he came forward again she pressed back against the wall, holding her skirt aside as if contact might contaminate. Then a shuddering sigh escaped as she watched him pick up the large tartan sponge-bag, hold it up in her direction as if to prove some point. For a split-second he smiled, but it faded as his attention was drawn to the wildly beating pulse in her throat, the agitated rise and fall of the scantily covered bosom.

'Oh, and, Briony——' he passed her and paused, one hand on the door-knob '—when I go I advise you to check that it's properly locked. If it had been any other man who had come barging in and caught you looking as you do now, especially with all that careful rear lighting——' when he smiled it was obvious he was under some quite intense strain '—I very much doubt if he would behave so honourably, foolishly some might call it, as I have. Whether he was married to you or not.'

The door closed behind him and she was left staring at the dark wood panels. Her legs were shaking and her head felt as if it belonged to someone else, but the most overwhelming sense

was one of grievous disappointment, and that
could never be explained.

'All that careful rear lighting' he had said, quite
as if she had deliberately stage-managed his re-
appearance. Tears stung her eyes. She turned,
extinguished the light with a sense of frustrated
grievance. And her hand, when she raised it,
shook so much she was barely able to slip the
bolt into position.

# CHAPTER THREE

It wasn't, she told herself reprovingly, as if the lightly covered male body was something new to her, the reverse in fact, since in her profession she had seen the lot, studied them from all angles and in every shape and size. Many shrunken with age and sickness, but also a surprising number of super-fit sportsmen suffering some temporary setback, recovering from a cartilage operation or desperate to repair a damaged back, all requiring the services of a sympathetic physio. But even while she could admire some superb physique she had always remained professionally detached to the extent that she had long imagined herself wholly impervious to any feminine flutterings.

Now, lounging at the edge of the pool, she had this absurd compulsion to watch, almost furtive under the protective cover of sunspecs and paperback book which she might be thought to be reading, and certainly with no understanding of why this one figure should be quite so intrusive. Maybe, she comforted herself, it was simple admiration for the powerful crawl, the incisive way he cut through the water, the sheer speed. So many things about the man she had married had been a surprise; the three days since their arrival in Provence had been a voyage of discovery.

This gorgeous house for one thing. When, a day or two before the wedding, allowing her no choice in the matter in his usual arrogant style, he had announced they would fly to France for a short break, he had given no indication that his own house was to be their destination. And she would never forget her first sight of it, all golden mellow stone in the late afternoon sun, the three Lombardy poplars which Finn told her he used as signals, the steady climb up the narrow winding road until suddenly the house vanished for a second before they swept on to the forecourt, drawing up on pale crunching gravel with layers of hillside falling away, disappearing into the distant haze which she was assured was the Mediterranean.

And the intimacy with Finn which she had dreaded so much had been comparatively easy; they were more like friends who had met by chance at an hotel, who were quietly appreciating each other's company when there was nothing more urgent on the agenda, but each free to follow any particular interest, in his case correcting proofs of the book which would accompany his next television series, and in hers the utter bliss of hours of light reading.

She had had no notion it would all turn out to be so restful; the very fact that she could recognise its therapeutic effects gave some indication of how taut and, yes... how tortured she had been in preceding weeks. Even the weather was playing its part; so early in the season it was positively balmy and...

Suddenly her attention was concentrated when the message reached her brain that Finn was heaving himself out of the pool, water draining from him, droplets shining on broad shoulders, clinging like sparkling crystal to the dark triangle of chest hair and... Hastily she lowered her eyes, fingers playing with an unread page, looking up with an affectation of surprise when he spoke.

'Don't know how you can resist.' Picking up a towel, lazily he rubbed down one arm and across his chest before dropping it and hooking a chair with his foot.

'Resist?' Nerves were wild, jangling. 'Resist what?' It was an effort to drag her attention away, up to his face. 'What do you mean?'

'Only——' a hand was thrust at the dark cap of hair, brushing it up and away from his forehead and he grinned, a heart-stopping flash of white. '*Only*——' it pleased him to emphasise the word '—what I said yesterday and the day before. Why don't you change and have a swim? The water's perfect, believe me.'

'Mmm.' She pretended to consider then stretched luxuriously, showing, though she was unaware of it, long slender legs faintly gold from the sun, arched foot, pink-painted toenails. 'But I'm simply enjoying this so much.' Her smile was stiff from the effort to be casual. 'Lying here soaking up the peace, it's idyllic. Besides, I'm not convinced——' ridiculous to imagine he might believe her with the paving stones throwing heat up at them, and she could feel a trickle of sweat down her backbone '—it *is* warm enough.'

'In that case——' his eyes searching hers seemed to be offering a challenge; there was something about the arched eyebrow, the curved mouth '—I may just have to prove it to you by whatever means present themselves.'

While she digested this he reached out for a jug of fruit juice, raised it invitingly then, when she shook her head, poured a single glass and took it to his lips. 'I shall have to push you in.'

'Don't you dare.' Voice not quite steady, she noted. 'If you do...'

'Relax.' Suddenly he rose, walked to the poolside and back, stood hands on hips demanding her attention. 'You are quite safe.' There was a sarcasm implicit in the tone more than the words themselves and at the same time a change of mood. The easy manner evaporated, became very nearly grim. 'I shan't... throw you in the deep end——' possibly he took pity on her when he saw the scald of colour in her cheeks, the nervous way her teeth caught at her lower lip '—till you let me know you are ready.' She knew the last thing on his mind, or on hers, was swimming, and drew in a shaky breath as she waited for him to continue. 'But——' unexpectedly he perched on the corner of her lounger, leaning forward so that his fingers almost grazed her legs; she struggled against withdrawing them

'—you do look better, Briony. Than when we arrived, I mean. More relaxed.'

Relief brought a faint smile to her lips; she was confident enough even to take off her dark glasses and lie back more easily in her chair, while she pointed. 'How could I be anything else in a place like this? It's heavenly, Finn.'

'*I* think so.' He followed the direction she was indicating before returning his attention to her face. 'It's my favourite spot in the whole world. And... I'm very choosy who I share it with. So you *are* glad you came?' Drily.

'Well...' What was there to say to such a question? Agreement might give entirely the wrong signals, but on the other hand...

'Not sorry?' he interrupted. 'Can one go that far?'

'Certainly not sorry.' With that she could agree wholeheartedly so long as he didn't imagine they were discussing anything other than the location. 'But maybe——' just for a moment she forgot her own feelings, wondered about his '—I suppose *you* could easily be sorry, Finn.'

'I was coming to that.' Her heart gave a quite violent thump of dismay; she had expected reassurance and now her eyes filmed over. 'I think it's important that we should talk...'

Of course it was, she thought dully; how could it be otherwise? It might be *easier* to coast along and trust that their problems could in some miraculous way be solved but...

'Yes.' She made no effort to hide her reluctance. 'If you like.'

'I think we must.' He sounded hard, much like the Finn whom she had so much resented on Edward's behalf, which was a good thing; she had been in danger of thinking the leopard had changed his spots, but if only it could have waited a little longer...

'This evening perhaps. I'm going to try to finish off those proofs right now.' Totally unaware of what he was doing, he allowed the back of his hand to rest for a moment against the bare sole of her foot and it was clear he did not share the intense reaction she experienced.

'Yes, of course.' Her reply was fairly calm, less strangulated than she had feared. 'If I can help you in any way...'

'No.' He smiled, the idea obviously one which afforded him some amusement, and he was right after all. What did she know about the sort of work he was involved with. But still...

'I might——' her hint of sharpness was a clue to a slightly bruised ego '—be capable of picking up some mistakes. I *can* spell, you know.'

'I'm sure you can.' Now he was being indulgent. 'And I'm the world's worst speller, but this clever machine I use does all my corrections.'

She didn't trouble to reply to that, her raised eyebrow was enough, and for a moment something shivered between them, left her breathless, exhilarated; it had about it a reminder of that moment when he turned towards her at the altar and...

'Right then.' He broke the tension, rose to his feet in a single fluid movement and in doing so brushed his fingers casually across her ankle. 'We'll meet later, then we'll talk.' And he didn't even glance at her as he crossed the terrace and disappeared into the house. Leaving her, nerves and emotions aflame, looking after him with an amalgam of resentment and longing which she didn't even try to identify. Instead, she leaned forward to soothe the spot he had touched, fingertips circling as if applying balm to scorched skin.

Late in the afternoon she woke with a start, sighed deeply as she put the still unread novel on the table beside her and struggled to her feet. The trouble about this sort of life, she assured herself as she stifled a yawn, was that it tended to make one lazy. But anyway, it was way past the time when they usually had some tea so she'd best go and fill the kettle. She slipped her feet into cork-soled sandals and walked slowly over to the open door into the cool hallway, then started as the main door opposite opened suddenly and the old-fashioned doorbell jangled a split-second later.

'Well now.' The young man standing in the open doorway seemed more at home than she was, and the girl who was a step behind and apparently responsible for the insistent ringing was equally familiar, judging by her grin. 'Well...you must be the bride.' He glanced behind. 'What would you say, Kitt?'

'I think you've hit the nail on the head.' A raised eyebrow and swift raking glance reminded Briony how hot and sticky and in need of a shower she was, her shorts and blouse a contrast to the girl's brightly patterned skirt and immaculate blouse. But before she could ask, in what would not have been a particularly welcoming voice, how she could help them she heard the sound of an upstairs door closing and then Finn was running lightly down the stairs, every inch of him, from the gleam in his eyes to the positive way he crossed the hall, showing pleasure, delighted no doubt to be relieved of the tedium of her undiluted society. Excluded for a few moments by the chatter and more especially by the way Finn greeted the girl, one, two, three cheek-to-cheek embraces was surely rather excessive. Even in Provence. More, now she came to count, than he had offered his wife...

So when he turned to make the introductions she made sure he was aware of her cool detachment. 'Briony, this is Kitt Lavery, her brother Clive Steading.' He was brief but probably felt compelled to drape an arm about her shoulder for a moment and to propel her in the direction of the kitchen. 'You came right on the dot; we often have tea about now.'

While she filled the kettle Briony was free to listen and to study. Clive was almost a dandy in a pale lemon suit, grey shirt and tie, suave, immaculate as if he had that moment emerged from Trumpers. And his sister was equally elegant, very blonde with her hair pulled severely back into a knot showing off a classical profile. But at least the talk confirmed that Finn had had no idea that they might be in the area; in fact had expected them to be in the States for at least another month.

'We have that rather nice white house at the bottom of the hill,' Kitt explained helpfully. 'I'm sure you'll have noticed it.'

Pausing in the act of setting out cups, Briony shook her head. 'No, we haven't been out since we came.'

'Ah,' Clive nodded. 'So are we to gather, Finn, you're keeping the girl strictly under lock and key?' and he laughed as he saw the hot colour in Briony's cheek.

'Something like that.' Finn smiled. 'We've had everything we need right here.'

'Well, I can *see* that. Thanks, Briony.' Clive took the cup she held out to him. 'I only hope we're not barging in on the honeymoon.'

'Well, you are, of course, but we're pleased to see you nevertheless.'

'Shut up, Clive, can't you see this is embarrassing Briony? Anyway——' Kitt smiled appealingly at Finn '—what we really came to ask is, is there any chance of the two of you joining us for a meal tonight? We weren't looking forward to St Miguel right now but the moment we got back old Georges came tapping at the door asking if we knew Monsieur Lawrence was here and that he had brought a brand-new wife with him. Of course we didn't, so he was more than pleased at the sensation he caused. *Alors,*' she ended with a little Gallic shrug, '*nous sommes ici.*'

'Georges,' Finn explained to Briony, 'is cousin to Lotti.'

'I see.'

'And we'll swop any time,' Clive chimed in. 'Lotti cooks much better than Georges gardens.'

'She *is* a wonderful cook——' impossible for Briony to disagree with that '—but today she has had to go off to visit a relative.'

'There you are, then.' Kitt seemed almost to think the matter settled. 'Couldn't have fitted in better. Is it agreed then, we make up a foursome, go down to the coast...?'

'Sounds like a good idea.' Finn directed his attention to his wife. 'What do you think, darling?' The last word, uttered in that casual, warm, very nearly convincing way caused an unexpected wave of emotion, tender at first, then when it registered how much of a sham it was, designed merely to impress his not very interesting friends, that was followed by a swell of anger. If that was the kind of game he wanted to play then she must not disappoint.

'As you say...darling.' Breathy, sensuous, indulgent, the long sooty lashes drooped over the striking eyes. 'It sounds like a wonderful idea.'

'Right.' For once Finn Lawrence was hesitant, his expression so speculative Briony thought she might have overacted, but his attention moved on to the visitors. 'I imagine you two are ready to go.'

'Well, we thought we could have a drink, watch the world go by before we eat; maybe we could dance later...'

'If that's the plan, then you'll have to excuse me.' Briony was glad of the chance to leave them; doubtless they would have plenty to talk about without her. 'I must have a shower, do something with my hair. I feel so sticky after lying all day in the sun.'

And she had few qualms about keeping them waiting while she had a leisurely shower before blow-drying her hair into one of her favourite styles. Come to think of it, fingers pushing it back over her ears, teasing a wispy fringe over her forehead—she was overwhelmed with sudden nostalgia—this had been a style Edward liked as well. 'Shows your perfect bone-structure, my love.' As she got up from the dressing-table and walked over to the wardrobe she could hear his voice as clearly as if he were in the room beside her.

And that might have explained why she didn't hear Finn knock at the bedroom door, why she was so startled when she saw his reflection in the mirror, was so suddenly aware that the satin camisole and briefs were more revealing than the bathing suit she had been so reluctant to wear.

The blouse she had just taken out offered a little protection when she held it against her but not enough. 'Don't you as a rule knock at bedroom doors before you barge in?' The amber eyes flashed molten warnings.

'Always.' Pointedly he pushed the door closed behind him, took three steps across the floor. 'Twice, in fact. I can't explain why you didn't hear.'

Briony swallowed, unable to explain why she wasn't dealing with this in a more adult way. He had after all given no sign of wanting to invade her privacy and...these days there was no big deal in the scantily clad female figure; certainly it was unlikely that he... 'Did you——' now he appeared to be concentrating his attention on the silver chain about her neck, the dangling bauble; it was almost as if he knew it was her present from Edward on her twenty-first birthday... '—did you want something?'

'Mmm.' At last his eyes returned to her face. 'I *did* want something.' Only it seemed he had no intention just then of explaining further.

'Yes?' Her voice was barely steady and for a moment it appeared he too was forced to try to concentrate his thoughts.

'Ah, yes.' There was a half-smile on his lips now, a faintly cynical gleam in his eyes. 'What I came to say was—don't feel you must agree if you don't want to—we——'

'Are you saying you would prefer to go on your own with Kitt and Clive?'

'No, you little fool, of course that's not what I'm saying.' Now there was a note of rasping irritation and she was pleased to have caught him on the raw. 'If you would let me finish, I was about to say, we were going to have that talk.'

'Oh, yes.' Forgetting what she was doing, Briony threw the silk shirt on to the bed. 'The talk. Well, it's all up to you. I shall fit in with whatever the rest want to do, don't mind me.'

'But I do mind, dammit.' He took a step towards her, the dark eyes ablaze with sudden anger. 'You're my wife, however much you might regret it, and how you behave is important to me.' His hands reached out to her shoulders, roughly at first, then spreading out over her skin as if he were wondering at the rich smoothness of silk. She shuddered; her eyes drifted closed as she tried to understand what was happening, this weakness in her stomach, a sweet fire in her pulses, and there was nothing she had the will to resist, rather the reverse, a desperate longing to drift with it, to let herself be swept away on a tide. The thin rouleau strap slipped from her shoulder and it hardly seemed to matter, until another tiny shake and she was released. 'And try to wipe that foolish sentimental look off your face,' he advised harshly. 'Forget about Edward Spurling. You're my wife and it's too late to wish otherwise.' He strode back to the door but she stopped him before he had time to put his fingers on the handle.

'But you can't stop anyone wishing, can you?' It wasn't what she had meant to say; especially she had not meant to invest the words with such blatant challenge. It was a particular matter for regret when she watched him turn, stroll slowly back so that he could look down from his considerable advantage. And she, refusing to appear intimidated, glared back, hoping he couldn't see the rapid tattoo of her pulses and knowing how ridiculous it was to try and challenge him dressed in a few wisps of silk and lace.

'There might be ways of doing just that.' If his voice betrayed a thread of amusement there was none in his eyes. 'Don't——' that word and its emphasis brought her mind back to the current discussion '—provoke me into an experiment, Briony.' A long pause as he allowed her time to absorb the veiled threat. 'Not at the moment, at least. You see——' taking the blouse from her nerveless fingers, he tossed it on to the bed and before she could retreat he had both hands about her waist '—You see——' his hands slid down over the thin silk panties, covering her hips, inclining her body into forceful contact with his '—I have promised myself a good deal of leisure when that precise time comes. Leisure and——' his eyes searched her face before coming to rest with blatant pleasure on her rapidly rising and falling breast '—and a certain degree of co-operation. The moment——' he smiled at her, then with one hand tipped her head back further '—is, I suggest, fast approaching.' And then, still holding her firmly, he lowered his head and touched his mouth to hers.

At least... that was her first impression of his intent. He had in the beginning meant simply to brush his mouth against hers but she, fool that she was, breathless and with her heart hammering wildly against the wall of her chest, allowed her lips to part in an attempt to ventilate; the soft pressure became bruising, tongues searched and touched. Briony felt she was being scorched; there was no strength in her legs and she collapsed on to the bed.

'No!' Crossing her hands over her chest, she lay there looking up at him and not entirely certain she meant what she said.

After a moment he repeated her denial with a touch of scorn which brought a wave of colour to her face. 'No?' The raised eyebrow, the faint smile were guaranteed to increase her shame and embarrassment. 'Well, maybe I agree with you. This isn't the moment, not with Kitt and Clive downstairs and wondering, coming to their own conclusions as to the delay. I'm sure they're more than halfway there already.' Seeing a renewed scald of colour, he shook his head cynically, 'Not everyone has your finer feelings, my sweet.' He walked towards the door, but just before he put out his hand for the handle he turned. 'Oh, and one last thing—I do trust you to put on a special show tonight, Briony. Clive and Kitt are old friends and I wouldn't like them to get a wrong impression about our relationship.'

'And if I don't?' Ridiculous to think she could
even begin to challenge a man who seemed to
hold all the aces.

'If you don't——' now he was deadly serious,
all pretence of lightness evaporating as he offered a warning she knew she could not afford
to ignore '—just remember how awkward it could
be when we meet up with your parents next week.'
The door closed behind him and she lay there for
a moment transfixed, then with a cry of anger
mingled with just a little self-pity she picked up
one of the cushions from the bed and hurled it
towards the door.

Put on a show. Inwardly repeating his words,
she strode about the room. Who did he think he
was to order her about like that? Scarcely coherent, she reached out for the blouse which he
had tossed so casually on the bed, began to slip
her arms into it then paused, all at once
thoughtful, then lips curling as the germ of an
idea came into her mind. If that was what he
wanted, then she might just do that. Put on a
show.

Swiftly she put the blouse back on its hanger.
Fingers searching, she brought out the chestnut
harem pants and sleeveless top, considered for a
moment, then she was hurrying, dressing, ad-
miring her reflection, pleased with the emphasis
on the length of her legs, the way the colour
brought out unexpected dark tones in her eyes
and...with some additional mascara, a few swift
touches with the brush, a different lipstick... She

was rushing now as she began to find some challenge in the situation; she searched through her handbag, finding what she wanted with a cry of triumph. Yes, it was perfect, all soft browns with pink undertones and a bronze sheen. Great. Grinning now, singing under her breath, such an unusual sound these days that she paused for a ridiculous moment trying to identify it, she searched in a drawer, found the woven gold belt which finished off her outfit, fastened it about her slender waist.

There now, she was almost ready. She slipped her feet into high mules, picked up her purse and walked to the door, returned to check herself in the mirror once more. Yes, it looked good, better than she would ever have imagined with its sensuous hints of Scheherazade and her bewitching tales. Even the dangling gold earrings she was wearing seemed appropriate and... Almost reluctantly she turned away, pausing only to blast herself extravagantly with her favourite Balenciaga perfume.

And then, supremely confident, she left the bedroom, head held high, not admitting even to herself exactly how stimulated and excited she felt, nor how provocative and impetuous she could be when the mood came on her.

He shouldn't, she told herself as she walked along the corridor, have set out to challenge her the way he had done. It was unforgivable of him to instruct her how she should behave in front of visitors. Perhaps his next suggestion would be that she enrol in some kind of finishing school when they went back to London; she could be Eliza to his Professor Higgins, she thought dramatically.

Reaching the stairs, she smiled down at the three people who stood there waiting, and began slowly to descend. A special show, he had demanded; well, then, a special show was what she was going to give. And Finn Lawrence was going to wonder exactly what had hit him.

# CHAPTER FOUR

NOT that there was any excuse for how things had gone later. She had meant to keep full control—this time she would be the one to call the tune—but...

What happened was down to so many things, all of which taken individually might have been irrelevant. For one there was the soft brush of silk against her skin, a sensation which made her aware of herself in an entirely new and exciting way. Or had that been the effect of an expression she had seen in Finn's eyes as she came down the staircase? The lazy, amused, but still very sensual look, full of dire hints and warnings totally at odds with the way he came forward and kissed her cheek. *That* was entirely for public consumption, like his, 'You look, and smell, quite wonderful my sweet.'

Which had left her pretty shaken, and when they reached the coast everything she experienced seemed planned to add new dimensions. The night air was soft and balmy, perfumed by miles of sweet herbs from the surrounding hills; along the quayside bobbed an entire flotilla of millionaire-style yachts with beautiful people coming and going.

She even found the companionship stimulating in spite of her earlier reservations, tried to forgive the way Kitt seemed to have appropriated Finn while she was left behind to walk with Clive. Then, the ambience of the tucked-away restaurant: delicious food, sparkling wine, her ridiculous satisfaction when she found herself sitting opposite her husband. Something about the unavoidable eye contact, the shared laughter, was disturbing and so very nearly hypnotic that she felt relief when the floor show began.

She thought she had never seen anything as exotic and exciting as the display put on by the Ukrainian Gypsy Troupe: dazzling colourful costumes, wild, athletic dancing, plaintive melodies played with heart-breaking tenderness by a trio of black-moustachioed musicians who wandered among the diners—one in particular who sang directly to Briony with a pleading expression in his shining coal-black eyes.

'Phew!' When he had moved on, Clive wiped his forehead jokingly. 'I really thought he was going to make you an offer, Finn.'

'Looked like that, didn't it? Only I should have wanted an awful lot of camels, and in any event I feel sure Briony would not have agreed to any sale.'

'Oh, I don't know.' She appeared to consider, looking towards the singer who seemed to be making a similar appeal at one of the other tables. 'I think he had something—they used to call it charisma.'

'Really?' Finn took her fingers, held them to his lips while continuing to look at her. 'Shall I call him back and negotiate?'

Blushing, she pulled her hand away, looking in embarrassment at Kitt and Clive who were smiling. 'Don't tempt me; it's only the thought of all those camels stopping me. Ukrainian camels, I've heard, are outrageously short-tempered, so how would you cope?'

Driving back to the villa soon afterwards, alone with Finn in his open-top coupé, the music ran persistently through her head, had the blood tingling again in her veins, and it wasn't till there was a hiss of tape that she realised the sounds were not after all imaginary. 'Finn.' Stretching sleepily, luxuriously, she slewed round in her seat and smiled. 'I thought it was all in my mind.'

'Not quite.' He grinned down at her. 'They were selling tapes, and since I could see you were so taken . . .'

'Yes, it was wonderful, so much colour and movement—I don't think I'll ever forget it. You were clever to bring the music with you; it will be a memento for always.' She stopped abruptly, struck by her implication that the evening was special enough to deserve one.

'Well, I did have a reason.'

'Oh?' Relaxing again, she leaned back, hands linked behind her head, face tilted so that she was staring directly up at the star-strewn sky. 'And am I allowed to ask what it is, this reason you mention?'

'Of course you're allowed to ask. But I'm not going to tell you.' Another laughing teasing glance in her direction. 'At least, not yet.'

'Oh,' she pouted, then entirely on impulse reached out a hand and touched the nape of his neck, trailing her fingers through the short hair. 'Anyway, thank you for taking me out tonight, Finn, I enjoyed it so much.'

'Me too.' His voice was so disturbingly deep and husky that she decided it was time for some detachment, so she swivelled round in her seat, caught a glimpse of a white house as they left the main road just as he pointed. 'That's where Kitt and Clive live.'

'Oh... I liked them both.' A pause. 'Has...Kitt ever been married? Although she and Clive are brother and sister, I notice she has a different name.'

'Yes, she was married once. Very briefly. She knew Tom was seriously ill before they married but their time together was tragically short, just four months. It took her a long time to get over it but now she's beginning to, although she doesn't care to talk a great deal about it.'

'I can understand that. Losing someone you love so much must be a terrible experience.' She paused, wondering if he might read into that remark much more than she had intended, but possibly not since they drew up in front of the house just then, and for no reason that she could see he took her hand to his mouth and dropped a quick kiss on the palm, releasing her before she had time to do more than draw breath, certainly showing no inclination to hold on to her. Then he was round, holding the car open and she was sliding out, but as she stood her high heel caught on a piece of gravel and there was a little stumble. For a reason she could not explain she turned the minor event into something of a drama.

'Steady.' His arms were about her in an instant, supporting her, gazing down into her eyes with a look of concern which the shadowy darkness seemed to intensify. 'Did you hurt your ankle?' His hands moved about her waist, and she felt her heart pump in excited agitation.

'No.' But her voice was trembly; she took a tentative step away, then... 'Ouch!' It was an excuse to grab at his arm, to prolong the moment of pleasurable excitement which was turned into a gasp, then an absurd little giggle as he swept her off her feet and walked towards the door.

'Finn, be *careful*,' as he shouldered the door aside. 'You might easily damage your back—I'm not exactly a lightweight, as you're probably realising.'

'Nonsense.' Inside the hall he allowed her to slip so that her toes were just in contact with the floor, arms still binding her closely. 'You're not much more than a featherweight.' Then he grinned as he made exaggerated gasping sounds which had her laughing in sympathy. 'Anyway, if I should put out my back surely this would be the perfect time.' His voice dropped a tone; he was so close and intimate that she was aware of his breath disturbing the tiny hairs on her skin, a sensation so urgent and erotic that she held her breath for fear of interruption. 'What more could I ask than to have my personal physio right here on the spot? I might even agree to a trade-in: accept the pain for a few blissful hours' treatment.'

The light from a single lamp in the far corner of the hall struck one side of his face, illuminating the strong lines, exaggerating the dark eyes which seemed to gleam with a new and still more forceful message, and then...and then, inevitable as night following day, his mouth touched hers, brushed once or twice—the bones in her body seemed to melt so that she became languid, incapable, content to be held still closer into the curve of his body, to enjoy the touch of hands as they slipped the length of her spine, to rejoice in the soft bruising pressure of his mouth on hers, allowing her lips to part as his grew more insistent and at last, in response to the clamour of her own pulses, to link her arms about his neck, listening to the rapid beat of his heart against her own, caring little that her tiny moaning cry was passing on a very particular message.

'It's all right.' His voice was low and laughter-laden; his chin nudged her cheek so that she had no choice but to look up at him, almost mesmerised by the glinting lights in the dark grey eyes. 'I think my back's going to be fine. Pity!' Smiling down at her, he supported her in the direction of the stairs. 'What about your ankle?'

Trusting the gloom would hide her guilty colour, she shook her head dismissively. 'Fine too.' She ought to have regretted her small deception getting out of the car but there was no point in trying to lie to herself and, by all the rules, they had left behind the moment for clear coherent reflection, for they had paused on the second step; his hands were linked possessively about her waist while she—she quite blatantly held up her face, inviting a replay of that scene in the hall, the one that had wrought such havoc on her self-control. At this rate it was going to take all night for them to reach the upper landing...

But in fact they were there quite soon, surrounded by the scents of dried lavender and other herbs overflowing from large stone pots in the window recess. They stood there, arms about each other, Briony at least willing the moment to last forever, but then Finn touched her skin again, both hands about her cheeks, fingers stroking lightly, eyes warm, tender. 'You know, you're a stunningly beautiful woman, Briony Lawrence.'

Lawrence? The shock of hearing the name caused her eyes to widen in surprise. 'Am I?' She sighed then, held her breath as he laughed softly, her mouth of its own accord beginning to share the joke.

'You know it,' he whispered as his arms came round her again and he buried his face in her hair. 'And you know where we're at, don't you?' The query gave her a jolt, one which lasted a mere second before her shoulders moved in a tiny acquiescent shrug; his arms slipped lower, moulding her still more closely to him and she had no notion of trying to escape.

'Your place or mine?' Dominant now, he looked down at her, ready to take what he wanted, and it was strange for her to acknowledge that now she was ready, impatient to give. And to take as well; it was all so mixed up— the giving and the taking seemed the same thing.

'Mine. If that's what you want.' Abandoned, that was how she felt as she issued the invitation, her mind fixed on that huge double bed, the downy pillows, a thick mattress where you could drown and...

Inside the room she had a moment's thankfulness that she had left it tidy—no wrinkled discarded tights or tossed-aside briefs to embarrass, only... What did she do now? Finn was coming closer; it was as if he could see into her mind, pick up on her uncertainty, for he was unfastening the gold belt about her waist, separating silk from silk, his hands caressing the skin of her back sending her mind spiralling out of control. She was incapable of dealing with this entirely novel assault on her emotions, but she knew she wanted to go on—there was no thought of stopping nor even of hesitation.

She watched Finn move away though his eyes were still fixed on her face. She saw him toss his jacket aside, begin to pull at his tie and then she, suddenly modest, turned away and began with shaking fingers to reach for fastenings, so inefficient that when Finn came to her, speaking quite gently, and again with that underlying note of amusement, and said, 'Let me help you,' she was happy to do just that.

Morning brought warm Provençal sun slatting in through the shutters and Briony lay for a moment of totally blank happiness, counting the stripes on the ceiling, watching a few dust motes drift on a rising current of warm air. Eyes began dreamily to close in idle contentment then flicked suddenly open as recollection returned. Another jolt when her hand brushing casually against her stomach encountered... nakedness. Insistent images intruded into her mind; her skin began to burn—surely these ideas were figments of her imagination, or...?

Tentatively, moving, stretching, her foot met up with...with another. She froze then; for what seemed like an age she lay scarcely breathing, immobilised, and in that instant the whole scenario of last night's performance, all its reality, unrolled—the whole, as they said, unexpurgated version.

Gingerly, with exacting wariness, she turned in the bed and found there exactly what she feared. Her husband was there, lying with his head on the pillow next to hers, one hand supporting his chin, the other extended so that it very nearly touched her shoulder. His breathing was regular, easy as a baby's....

Briony lay there staring, colouring up again as further details returned. Had she really behaved with so much abandon? How could she expect him to believe she was inexperienced except... except that he was bound to know...? And, knowing, he had behaved with the utmost gentleness, with a consideration and restraint she would hardly have believed fitted in with the positive, dynamic character of Finn Lawrence. All of which went to show how impossible it was to make judgements about people until you knew them with some degree of intimacy. Which she could now claim. Hot colour surged over her cheeks as she remembered.

Then as he stirred in the bed she held her breath, at the same time looking at him with a wholly unexpected stab of something that felt like tenderness. He looked so much more vulnerable than the Finn Lawrence she was used to, younger in spite of the darkness of the beard showing through. Ridiculous eyelashes—she resisted the inclination to put out a finger to touch gently. Not for the world would she wake him, in fact... She lay back carefully and, still looking at him, considered. It would be best if she could slip out of bed without waking him, have a shower and... She didn't quite know what she would do after that but something would occur to her.

Reaching out for the side of the bed to pull herself upright, she was suddenly, quite unexpectedly, arrested by an iron bar descending from nowhere and pinning her back into position.

'Where do you think you're off to?' A voice was growling in her ear, an arm pulling her into a position which was too intimate by far.

'Oh, Finn.' Cheeks ablaze, she looked at him. 'Good morning,' quite as if they had met in the Underground.

'Good morning,' he mocked, but softly. Come to think of it, she would never have believed a man like Finn Lawrence could be so gentle and so... Something about his eyes made her still hotter. 'How are you?' His fingers were describing little circles in a very sensitive area of her diaphragm.

'I'm fine, Finn. Only——' ineffectively she stretched, trying to see the clock on one of the tables '—I must get up, I'm sure it's getting late.'

'There's all the time in the world.' He showed no sign of giving in to her. 'After all, this is exactly what honeymoons are for.'

'Yes, I know,' she blurted out, 'but this one was meant to be different.'

'Was it?' He eased himself into a still more comfortable position. 'Was it really? I didn't realise...' And he was close enough to trail kisses down her throat. 'But I'm not complaining.'

'You know it was.' Panic was beginning to rise inside her, panic helped not at all by the light touch on her thigh. She tried to lean back but even that was offering him still more scope for... 'And you know last night we were meant to be talking, about the future I mean, and not going out on the town with Kitt and Clive.'

'Ah, yes.' Of course he was toying with her. 'I believe I do remember.' And without doubt he was judging accurately her reaction to every little move he made, the casual brush of a finger across her throat, drifting down to her breast and . . . all the wild and mind-blowing sensations she had experienced last night were back and hammering for attention . . .

'Finn, will you let me go? Please?' she wailed as the remnants of her resolution began to slip away from her. 'Please, Finn.'

'You know you don't mean that. Besides, I think now is maybe the time when we should have our talk. If that indeed is what you want, and it's unlikely we shall have such a perfect opportunity, such total privacy.'

'So . . . all you want to do is talk.' The scorn she intended to muster came out sounding like a coy invitation.

'Not *all*! But I've no objection to a *little* talk before we go on to something more interesting. If that is what you really want.'

'Lotti will think . . .' It was almost her last card.

'Lotti will think what we're doing is entirely natural. She would be desperately disappointed if we were to continue as we have until now. Eleven o'clock will be quite time enough for us to show our faces. Besides . . .' His hand came from beneath the covers and reached for the back of her head, so powerful, so insistent that she put out both her own hands to thwart him. And encountered the warm chest, the thick sprinkling of shiny hair which last night had given such inexplicable delight and even now . . . Beneath the sensitive fingertips it was easy to pick up the powerful, insistent beat of aroused desire and . . . and her own senses were under such very determined assault that she was rapidly losing any ability to resist. 'Besides——' against her cheek his voice was hurried '—you know you want it quite as much as I do . . .'

And she, with her mind spiralling out of orbit, lacked the capacity to argue and what was more, if she were being honest, she would have been forced to admit that any desire to do so had long since been side-tracked.

'You know . . .' With his teeth nibbling at her earlobe, still in the drowsy aftermath of lovemaking, she had no inclination to move away from the strong arms holding her; in fact, if he continued along these lines, she could foresee that they might still be here at lunchtime. 'We needn't . . .'

'Mmm?' As she moved her head on the pillow, burrowing a little deeper, his mouth came into contact with her closed eyelids, and her hands traced the contours of his chest for a moment's further pleasure before settling about his waist, edging a little closer.

'Ah, yes.' He was husky, breathless. 'Oh, yes, I do agree with that. Mmm.' And he feathered kisses over both eyes, down her cheek till he reached her mouth.

'You were saying?' A desperate attempt on her part to control the situation, to return it to some level of calm detachment.

'What?' Looming above her he showed no sign of interest or co-operation.

'You were saying something...' Her head fell back, allowing unlimited scope and encouragement. 'You said...something like...we needn't...'

'What I was going to say was, we needn't go back home in two days as we planned...'

'Two days?' Shock jerked her back to reality with more speed than she would have believed possible, dismay sounding in her voice, indignation in the way she searched his face for confirmation. 'But surely...'

'Yes, I agree with you, the first few days were simply thrown away, but what I'm saying is, we can cancel our flights and take them up later.'

'But I'm due back at——'

'We could do our best to make up for those lost days.' Gently he brushed back a strand of hair from her forehead. 'Think of it—lazy hours spent at the pool, after lunch a siesta, then if you would prefer we could go into town to eat—you might even meet up with the camel-master again.'

She couldn't suppress her snort of laughter which she followed with a mockingly shaken fist. 'As I said before, don't tempt me; I might just...'

'Let's not waste time talking about him. Just tell me, what do you think of my brilliant idea?'

'Well, all your ideas are brilliant, you know that.' The little edge of sarcasm was a defence against her own treacherous inclination. She was swept by a scarcely resistible longing to forget everything, to abandon all her responsibilities and give in to his suggestion. Her brain was pretty near numbed by the prospect, but instead she fought against it as if the devil himself was tempting her. Her sigh was long and deep, a reflection of an overwhelming sense of loss which she could not have explained even if she had been aware of it. 'I can't. You know that.' For a second close to tears she sniffed, blinked. 'You know I had trouble getting time off even for the wedding. It has meant a heavy load on the whole department so... I'd better go back. But you——' the thought was expressed before she had time to consider '—if you really want to stay on, there's no reason why you shouldn't——'

'Thank you.' He spoke through clenched teeth and rose quite suddenly, standing on the floor, hands on hips, glaring down at her in the tumbled bed. It was clear he was in a fury, but even while she tried to explain this to herself she was affected by the powerful strength of that dark taut body, the width of shoulder, the narrow hips and...

'Wh... what?' Wrenching her eyes back to his face she coloured guiltily. 'What did I say?'

'You invited me to let you go home alone while I presumably stop on here for the rest of the honeymoon.'

'I . . . I didn't mean it like that. I just thought, since Clive and Kitt are here you might want to see them . . .'

'And who, I wonder——' quite unselfconscious, he reached out for the trousers he had discarded the previous night and stepped into them, pulling the belt about his waist, each move invested in some way with his potent sense of outrage '—who is there in London whom you might want to see, Briony? I think that is closer to the nub of the problem.'

'I merely——' it was hard to raise a defiant chin lying in bed but she tried '—was thinking of what would be best for you. As far as I'm concerned, I have no plans for meeting anyone at all.' It was only then that she caught the drift of his question, felt her skin grow hot, and knew she was exhibiting all kinds of guilt signals. At the same time she was outraged and wounded that he should even think she might seek out Edward . . .

'I'm sure you haven't.' His cynical tone indicated an entirely contrary conviction. 'Now, if you don't mind, I'll go and have a shower. I'll see you downstairs . . .'

For some time Briony lay without moving, trying to control the tears which were struggling to escape, and then with a bound she rose from the bed, sniffed once or twice before reaching for a handful of tissues from the box on the dressing-table. The sight of her naked body leaning forward caught her attention; slowly she straightened up, searching the image for some

clue that made her so entirely different from the
person she had been yesterday.

And found none. Face, hair, neck, none of
them betrayed any secrets, even the lips which
had been kissed and plundered until they stung
and throbbed looked very much as always,
perhaps very slightly swollen. Moving closer she
was surprised to see the mouth curve as if re-
flecting on certain pleasures. She grew impatient
with herself, picked up a towel, shrugged herself
into a robe and made for the adjoining bathroom.

It was crazy, all this introspection; she had
made a mess of things in more ways than one
and she simply had to face up to the conse-
quences of her own actions. Only... As she
rubbed shampoo into her hair, held her face up
to the warm sting of the shower, her mind insisted on returning to one disconcerting and very
humiliating thought. It was something Finn had
teased her about during one of the sessions of
foreplay just an hour or two ago. Why was it that
she, so totally inexperienced, should have res-
ponded with such complete enthusiasm, behaved
with such lack of inhibition?

How was it, in short, that she, Briony Maxwell,
had taken part so wholeheartedly with Finn
Lawrence? Where, she asked herself with something approaching disillusion and despair, where
in heaven's name did love fit in?

## CHAPTER FIVE

THEIR last full day before returning home turned out to be surprisingly enjoyable. Finn recovered from his irritation—that was one thing she had come to recognise: though from time to time he had a short fuse, it burned fast and furious and went out as suddenly as it had ignited—and declared he had done as much work as was necessary and that it would be a good idea to take a picnic and explore some of the country round about.

The weather continued balmy and idyllic while they drove along quiet country roads, visited a *parfumerie* near Grasse, lingered in the old town and market before driving on to a small lake where they opened the basket Lotti had prepared for them.

'Mmm. I was hungry and these are delicious.' Briony popped a last morsel of pastry into her mouth. 'Shrimp, I think, with some kind of herb, and the others are onion, garlicky. I must ask Lotti for the recipe.'

'She'll be pleased if you do.' Finn held out a glass of the wine he had just poured. 'She's extremely vain about her cooking.'

There was a pause while they ate and drank contentedly, watching unseen fish making widening ripples on the smooth surface of the water. 'So she ought to be. Has she been looking after the house for a long time?'

'Since I can remember. The house belonged to my parents. It was...' He hesitated and appeared to be looking into the far distance. 'It was about the only thing that didn't disappear into a black hole after the accident. Probably because it was outside the UK and...no one could get their hands on it,' he ended on a note of bitterness.

'Oh?' Until now he had shown little inclination to talk of his parents, which had not affected her curiosity; now she took the opportunity he offered. 'It was a skiing accident, wasn't it?'

'Yes.' A longish pause. 'When I was sixteen. In fact, I would have been with them except I went down with some virus which was rampaging through school. They were going to cancel but I persuaded them to go off without me; it was only a five-day break and they had been working so hard...'

'Oh, Finn. How awful for you.' Sympathetically she held out her hand, and was pleased when he linked his fingers through hers and held them against his cheek for a moment.

'Devastating. They were both such wonderful people; I can never explain how much I've missed them through the years.'

'Your mother—that picture in your sitting room—she looks so beautiful. So alive. Does that sound silly?'

'No, it's what she was. Both of them, they lived life to the full. If it hadn't been for that freak accident they would have been alive now. If...if...if! There were strange weather conditions—they think a sudden roll of thunder started off a series of avalanches. It was all over in seconds. Two other skiers were killed, another was pulled out barely alive.'

'And afterwards?' After a long pause she asked, 'Was it then that you came to spend your holidays with...with Ed...with the Spurlings?'

'Mmm.' His manner hardened noticeably. 'My mother and Aunt May were stepsisters and Sir Julian joined my parents' company two years before the accident.'

'You...you don't like him, do you?'

'Not a lot. Aunt May is all right but totally dominated by him. I suspect she finds it easier that way. He's a very confident, brash individual, something of a bully. I spent two holidays with them, and after that decided to make other arrangements.'

About to query his relationship with Edward, she changed her mind. It was all too recent, too raw right now, and besides...

'Anyway——' releasing her hand he smiled, lay back on the rug, eyes closed, crossed hands supporting his head '—it was all a long time ago.'

Yes.' Silly to feel rejected simply because he was signalling the end of the subject, and crazy... Surely she couldn't be jealous, not of a relationship which so closely resembled hers with her parents except... Since they had died so young, it would never be challenged, the ties could never be loosed by other different ties, and...

Slowly she began to replace some of the picnic remains in the basket, opened her mouth to ask Finn if he had finished with his wine, and saw his breathing had become more regular, lips parted in relaxation.

So much had happened, her whole life turned upside down in...less than six weeks. And here she was, coping with what would have been unimaginable while the man she loved... Well... She didn't even know what Edward meant to do. Would he marry Pamela or not? And...she felt very much distanced from that and—her long fingers plaited and unplaited the fringes of the tartan rug—much more involved in her marriage to this man who was a virtual stranger.

Beneath lashes, afraid that he might suddenly flick back his eyelids and surprise her, she watched him and felt her heartbeats begin to pick up some of her tensions as she remembered what had happened between them last night. And again this morning. If anyone had forecast it she would never have believed them, and it was her own reaction which was more of a puzzle than his. Life—she sighed deeply, laced a hand against her ribcage—life was so complex, beyond anyone's comprehension. Best to give up trying to make sense of it all...

She lay back looking up at one or two fleecy clouds moving idly against the sky, but the image of the man she had married would not be excluded. He was, after all—and for the first time she was prepared to admit it—cast much more in the role of romantic hero than the one she loved so intensely. High-profile, successful, attractive to women, she knew that from the reaction of most of the female staff at St Barnaby's when they heard her news. Drooling envy was commonplace, with lack of comprehension from some.

'What on earth have you got, Maxwell, that the rest of us have missed out on?' one very glamorous staff nurse had demanded with less than wholehearted generosity.

'You'll have to ask Finn that,' she had joked, though she would have welcomed an answer herself, even if it did raise more problems than it solved.

It was annoying that on the way home they came on Clive, who was mowing the strip of grass that lay along the side of their house.

'I was looking out for you two.' He mopped his forehead with a spotted handkerchief. 'We saw you drive off this morning but couldn't catch you. Kitt wonders if you'd like to come and join us for the first barbecue of the season.'

'Mmm. Sounds like a good idea. I don't think Lotti will have started on our evening meal yet. What do you say, Briony?'

Which of course left her little choice but to feign pleasure and agree, though driving the few hundred yards up to the house she indulged herself in a little litany of silent complaint. Don't they understand that we're on our honeymoon? And don't they realise we have a thousand and one personal problems to tackle before we can begin to sort our lives out?

But as things turned out it was a pleasant evening, much more low-key than the previous one. They ate delicious grilled meat with garlic bread and salad, drank moderately one of the local wines, the ongoing easy conversation giving Briony an insight into their neighbours' lives which she had previously lacked.

Clive, she learned, was divorced from his American wife but he had a son at UCLA. 'We're all good friends,' he assured Briony, who had helped him carry some of the dirty dishes into the kitchen, 'just don't want to live together.'

'You get on better with your sister than a wife?'

'Seems to work like that, and of course we do spend a great deal of time apart. Often I'm in the States when she's in London. And I often take the chance of a quick trip to California to see Adam and his mother.'

'Sounds like the best of both worlds.'

'Well, I'm glad Sylvie and I had Adam before we split up. I shan't marry again, and most men like to think the family name is being continued.'

'Most men are vain enough, I agree with you.'

'Miaow.' He grinned at her, then swung round as Finn came in from the garden. 'The kitten has claws.'

'I've found that out already.' His eyes were dark and perceptive, the faint smile curious. 'What has she been saying to you, Clive?'

'I'll leave her to tell you that.' And picking up a board of cheeses he made for the door, leaving his guests to follow.

A little later, when Briony was having difficulty keeping her eyes open, it seemed time to go and she yawned and apologised as she was saying her goodnights.

'There you are.' Clive grinned mischievously. 'The bride is exhausted. Go home, Briony, and sleep.'

'I promise to do just that.' In spite of burning cheeks she was less embarrassed than might have been expected, and smiled as they drove up the lane. 'Oh...' Stretching out her arms, she stifled another yawn. 'There is something about this place. Something magical.'

'Mmm.' A quick sideways glance which she was aware of. 'You've discovered that quickly.'

'Yes.' Determined to be prosaic, she pushed herself up in the seat. 'I blame the wine. I'm not used to drinking so much. It's bound to be very corrupting.'

'I don't think you need worry, not with the amount you drink.' They turned in through the stone pillars and crunched up the drive. 'You and Clive seemed to be getting on well.'

'Yes, I like them both. He was telling me about his son in the States. Sad that he's divorced.'

'Oh...I think it suits them best that way. Now...' Pulling up, he was quickly out of the car and opening her door. 'Come on, let's walk round the garden for the last time. It's a pity to waste such a balmy evening, and remember, back to earth and London with a bump tomorrow.'

'Yes.' The reminder caused quite a pang, and she allowed her hand to stay in his as they wandered down the path and stood by the pool on stones still warm from the heat of the day.

'I didn't realise...' His voice was soft and dreamy, beguiling in a way that brought the blood pounding in her veins, made her catch her breath and try to grab at some self-control. He was turning her to face him, circling her with his hands. 'I didn't realise you had such a tiny waist.'

'No?' The coquettish note shocked and surprised her—it was a warning that any ideas of self-defence were rapidly evaporating. 'And when did you first notice?' Her heart was hammering against her ribs, just above his hands. If he moved his thumbs...

'Oh——' that intonation, lazy and mellow, might have been designed with seduction in mind '—maybe when I saw you coming up the aisle in church, all cloudy and beautiful, your hand holding the flowers shaking just a little, and then I noticed...' She had been drawn closer, his breath was warm against her cheek. 'I confirmed it...last night...again this morning.' She felt the

touch of lips on her skin, moved her head a
fraction, not deliberately offering hers... 'And
I mean to keep on checking...' Her lips parted
in blatant invitation, the soft bruising pressure
increased... 'I don't suppose I could persuade
you...'

It was a moment before her mind cleared. Was
he offering her a chance to...? 'What?' Hard to
believe it was possible...

'Don't you think——' his voice was full of
laughter '—don't you think before we go back
you should... try the pool?'

'Now?' Her relief was overwhelming; she
sounded breathy and very nearly encouraging.
'But I haven't got my...'

'What does that matter?' Obviously taking her
reply for agreement, he was busy dealing with
the buttons on her white lawn blouse, unfastening the wide elastic belt, one garment after
another was tossed on to the tiled floor, but while
she still had the protection of bra and briefs she
kicked aside her high sandals, and a few swift
steps were followed by a smooth dive into the
water. She touched the bottom, pushed herself
back to the surface and drew one quick breath
before dominating arms, powerful legs encircled
her, pulling her down as their mouths met, and
as his fingers dealt with the last fastenings she
experienced a sense of freedom which was
pure hedonism.

*    *    *

'Aaah.' An endless sound of satisfaction broke from her lips as she stirred sleepily and turned on to her side, smiling as her hands traced the length of one thigh then came up to measure the narrowness of her waist. 'Aaah,' she sighed again as certain images of the previous night returned. Who could have thought a hot shower would offer such pleasure? Of course—her lips curved still more complacently at the recollection—it was the first time she had shared . . .

And even afterwards, wrapped in his warm towel robe, drinking hot chocolate while drying her hair lying on the rug in front of an electric fire . . . And what came after, when he carried her back to the bedroom, she would never, ever have believed . . . Sleep began to reclaim . . .

'Must we——' his mouth was even now travelling the length of her cheek, stopped beside her mouth while his hands . . . Half-heartedly she caught at them '—must we, do you think, Briony, really go back today?'

'We must.' No matter how he cajoled, she felt duty-bound to go back to work. 'But not yet; it's still early.' She snuggled more deeply among the covers. 'And sleep, remember.' Impossible to conceal the smile of reminiscence. 'That was what Clive said, and yet you persist . . .'

'And you . . .' His mouth was on hers, forceful, gentle, bewilderingly potent in the way it coaxed her lips to part. 'You loved it. Confess.'

'Mmm.' Her sense of pleasure, of eager impatience, was dimming her sense of discretion,

making her careless. 'Isn't it strange, Finn. I
never dreamed it would be like this, that sex on
its own could be such sheer intense pleasure. So
pleasurable.' Her tongue savoured the sound of
the word as much as her memory did the act. 'So
wonderfully...perfect. So sensual.' Uncon-
scious that the fingers circling her breast had
grown still, his mood of relaxation and indul-
gence had become taut, she allowed her half
dreaming thoughts expression. 'I would never
have believed it could be so perfect in the ab-
sence of some pretty strong emotional
attachment.'

His silence, an unexpected atmosphere of
tension and strain, made the heavy eyelids flicker
then sweep back in time to see him standing by
the side of the bed, looking down at her with a
cold, bleak anger which made her shiver.

He strode to the door, a dark, magnificent and
at that moment dangerous animal. 'You're quite
right, of course, it is time to go back. Possibly
it was, after all, a mistake to come.' The door
closed, but not quickly enough entirely to damp
out his final words which sounded suspiciously
like, 'Damn you, Briony.'

For a moment she lay quivering on the bed,
unable to understand why the mood had so
quickly changed from euphoria to black and
abject misery. And then her own words were
sounding in her ears, and she understood how
much reason he had for his anger. A few tears
came and she allowed them to run down her

cheeks, into her ears and on to the pillows. But then, seeing the futility of it, she decided there was nothing for it but to get up. She had her packing to do after all and . . .

Stepping from the bed, she was forced to confront her reflection in a mirror, and she stood there for a moment, allowing her fingers to touch a few spots specially sensitive to Finn's touch. There was even the hint of a tiny bruise where she had caught his fingers, pressing them to her in an excess of impatience and excitement. He had brought her, it would be mad to deny it, an intensity of pleasure and fulfilment which she had never dreamed of, which she was pretty sure no other man could . . . No, not even with Edward would she have reached such a pitch as she did with Finn.

Of course, most people put it down to simple chemistry; with some couples it was just there even though . . . And other people who loved each other desperately missed out on it. What was it Finn had asked her way back, that first evening after the disastrous party at Duncan Harraby's? He had suggested, infuriating her at the time, that since she had been able to resist Edward's persuasions and with comparative ease, perhaps they were not so idyllically suited as she imagined.

But now, if he should repeat such an assertion, she would have to consider. Certainly, much of her conviction had evaporated. Where once upon a time she could not have imagined enjoying an intimate relationship with a man she didn't love

madly and wholeheartedly, she recognised that
the truth of it was much more complex. Now she
was on the verge of deciding ... Oh, it was just
too ridiculous, pointless to spend so much time
on a problem which was difficult to resolve,
only...she did regret making such a crass remark
to Finn, especially when he had been responsible
for taking her to a quite new emotional di-
mension. She had been thoughtless and unkind,
and even the fact that she had been half asleep
was no real excuse.

It would be awful if she had damaged what
they had found together; tears pricked at the back
of her eyes at the thought. No matter that the
rest of their life might have its problems, it was
idle to pretend to herself that she and the man
she had married were not entirely and gloriously
compatible in one important aspect at least. And
she knew now she would value that the more,
simply because she had denied its existence for
so long.

# CHAPTER SIX

BACK in London they came into contact with a spell of unseasonably cool weather, a shock after the mellow Provençal days but seeming in some way to find an echo in Briony's mood. It was a good thing, she reassured herself, that she was being kept so busy at St Barnaby's as well as with her private patients, and this, added to all the trauma and disruption of clearing her things out of her flat and moving into Finn's home, left little time for personal analysis.

Some instinct—privately she blamed the sluggish state of the housing market—inclined her towards letting the flat, not selling which was Finn's advice, so she was pleased when, a day or two after her return to work, Julie, slightly embarrassed and apologetic, hinted that she might be in the market for renting.

'But I thought——' they were sitting in the staff dining-hall and Briony looked up from her coffee, eyebrows raised '—I always thought you were happier sharing with Beth and Naomi.' The three ward sisters had known each other since probationer days. 'Safety in numbers, you always said. Besides...' Awkward to suggest she might not be able to afford the rent.

'Well, you see——' Julie was very busy with her Danish pastry '—you know I told you at the wedding that Nigel and I were...' Here she made a little rocking movement with one hand, looking up with a sudden grin. 'He wants us to move in together.'

'Ah, I see.' Nigel was a recently arrived houseman who had been dating Julie for some time. 'I thought when I saw you dancing together at the wedding...' Briony pursed her lips in mock disapproval. 'But what will Mama say?'

'With luck the parents won't know.' She sipped and dabbed her mouth with a tissue. 'And if anyone should tell them...well, I'll just have to say that most women my age have long since succumbed to what is pretty well par for the course now. In fact, you're about the only person I know who didn't cohabit before the wedding.' Watching the blush spread over Briony's face she grinned relentlessly...

'It's you we're talking about,' said her friend weakly.

'Yes, well, just because my father chose to go into the church it doesn't mean I, his only child, must live like a nun.'

'Oh, I don't know. You have done until now.' And they both giggled. Having spent so many hours sharing their views on life and love, each seemed to know instinctively how the other felt.

'Yes.' Julie's pretty face suddenly changed. 'And look where that's got me—almost at the back of the shelf. I know it's wrong, but when I look at you I feel madly envious...'

'At me?' Briony felt her jaw drop. 'What on earth do you mean?'

'Well, in case you didn't know...' Smiling again, teasing, Julie leaned forward, elbows on the table, cup supported between her hands. 'Not only did you capture just about the dishiest man around but you came back from a few days in France quite transformed. Yes, blush as much as you like but everyone has noticed. I won't embarrass you further by telling you what old Mr Lucas thinks has worked such a change—he went into quite a bit of graphic detail.'

'Julie!'

'OK, OK, but there is a glow about you which wasn't there before and which is surely down to the Hunk. Oh, I know you try to subdue it but it's difficult to hide, and I think it's time for me to sample a slice of whatever is on offer.'

'Well.' Briony determined to ignore the implications, to concentrate on the main issue. She had reservations about Nigel, who was the kind of young doctor who made a career of appropriating the prettiest nurses, regarding it very much as his right, and who would move on without hesitation if someone new appeared on the horizon. 'So long as you're sure, Julie. About Nigel, I mean—it is a bit sudden, after all.'

'Sudden, she says. The one who barely gave me time to have a bridesmaid's dress made, to choose a present.'

'That was different.' Smiling through a wave of colour, Briony stuck to her opinion. 'I'm a respectable married woman, entitled to dish out advice.'

'Yes, yes.' An impatient wave of Julie's hand dismissed the lecture. 'But tell me——' voice and manner became more confidential '—I don't mean in detail, I don't expect that. But I bet Finn is a fantastic lover. Oh, dear.' Clapping her hand over her mouth, she affected regret. 'I'm embarrassing you—myself too, I shouldn't have asked that. But he is, isn't he?'

'What do you expect me to say? If I said you were wildly wrong, I don't suppose you'd believe me.'

'From that answer I shall draw my own conclusions, but you're quite right, I wouldn't believe you. You see, I've noticed the soft gleam in your eyes, the way your lips smile when you imagine no one is looking.' Ridiculously she 'played' a few bars on a non-existent violin. 'But seriously, what about the flat, Briony, is there any chance . . . ?'

'Of course you can have it if you want.' She knew the rent would be entirely within the means of two sharing and, almost as important, that Julie would be a careful tenant.

'Brilliant. Bless you.' Rising, Julie drained her cup. 'Now I must dash. I might just catch Nigel if I get my skates on. I hardly dared hope—I was so convinced you'd be putting the flat on the

market now that you and Finn are so cosily
settled ... oh, and give him my love, won't you?'

And putting the flat on the market, Briony reflected soberly as she made her way back to her
department, was exactly what Finn imagined she
was doing. And it was going to be difficult to
explain to him her reasons for doing anything
else. Come to that, she was reluctant to delve too
deeply herself, half afraid of the answer she
would be forced to contemplate.

Since coming back from France, a sense of
constraint had developed between them. Finn was
withdrawn and remote, and Briony felt herself
to be in the position previously reserved for
Edward. And she found being the focus of disapproval was something she resented even more
than when it had been directed at his cousin.

They had spent that first Saturday · morning
ferrying personal things from the flat to the
house. 'So when are you thinking of selling?'

'I'm not sure.' Turning away, she placed a pile
of papers on a shelf in the wardrobe. 'I haven't
quite made up my mind.' In a desire to be
awkward she had, when given the choice, chosen
as their bedroom the one with twin beds, a decision he had accepted without comment, yet
another source of irritation for Briony. It might
have been better she thought mutinously, to have
gone the whole way and insisted on separate
rooms ... If only she'd had the nerve she could
have saved herself a whole lot of *Angst*. Watching
him, covertly of course, strolling about the room

wearing little more than a towel—well, it did cause a certain amount of frustration, was bound to, and she couldn't understand why he showed no sign . . .

'You *are* intending to sell it, I suppose?' She hadn't noticed him moving to block her way as she turned from the cupboard. His hands came up to grip her shoulders.

'I said——' she spoke through gritted teeth; not for the world would she have admitted the effect his touch, ungentle as it was, was having but she knew that in any clash with such a dominating man she must adhere to her own views or go under '—that I had not yet decided. When I do make up my mind——' she broke away, making a great show of concentrating on the clothes she was unpacking '—you shall be the first to know, I promise.'

And now, remembering that promise, she realised she had just broken it, but still she felt ridiculously nervous of telling him. Certainly today was the wrong time; with her parents coming on their first visit it was no time to pre-cipitate an argument. And thinking of that, she must remember to go and pick up the chocolate gâteau ordered from the Viennese *Konditorei* on the corner of Park Street. Finn had, surprisingly, offered to provide the main course if she would do the first and the pudding.

'Darlings, it's lovely to see you so settled and looking so happy.' Jane Maxwell lay back in her chair, looked round the dining area with some satisfaction and sighed. 'Obviously married life suits you both, don't you agree, Tony?' she appealed to her husband.

'Yes, for the third time.' His sigh was a shade more weary. 'But don't go on about it, love, you're making your daughter blush.'

'No, I'm not,' Briony lied quite blatantly as she began collecting plates then, catching Finn's eyes, she smiled and was stirred to slow delight by the responsive gleam in his eyes. For a split-second they might have been isolated until she remembered her parents. 'I married him for his cooking, you know.' An intercepted amused glance between her parents increased her confusion. 'He's an expert on all kinds of exotic foods—quite shows me up, as you must now realise.'

As she hurried towards the kitchen she heard her mother make some remark about the lamb with couscous and then add, 'And after dinner we have a surprise for you both.' Briony paused at the door, saw her mother touch her handbag. 'In here.'

'A surprise.' Finn followed her into the kitchen with the vegetable dishes. 'Sounds ominous.'

Deep down Briony too had a sense of foreboding, only she wasn't about to admit as much. 'Would you get the gâteau out of the fridge, and the bowl of whipped cream? Top shelf.'

'How's your video, Finn?' When they had
settled in the sitting-room, Jane reached positively for her handbag.

'The video?' He handed his mother-in-law the
drink she had asked for. 'It's fine. Why do you
ask?'

'Because——' she produced a flat package and
waved it triumphantly '—because I happen to
have with me the recording of the wedding of the
year, Great Denlow style.'

Oh, *no*. For a moment Briony was afraid she
might have spoken aloud, and sighed with relief
when there was no surprised reaction. A quick
glance towards Finn showed him to be impassive, and she had no choice but to lay on some
false enthusiasm. 'Oh, how wonderful,' she said,
and actually sounded sincere.

'Well, here it is, Finn. You'll be more expert
than I am at setting it all up, and to be honest
we're dying to see it ourselves. You can sit
together on the sofa, and don't mind us if you
want to hold hands.'

But they didn't, though Briony could hardly
have been more aware of her husband if they had
been locked into intimate body contact.

As it was, her attention was more on the dark
hand resting on a cushion, occasionally moving
to pick up a glass, more on the sprinkle of dark
hair under the heavy gold watch bracelet than on
what was happening on the small screen.

Until all of a sudden there she was, dewy and
romantic, unbelievably glamorous in the doorway

of the family home, laughing with her father as they tried to restrain the cloud of veiling caught in a tiny breeze. And she had been wrong, she decided with a little indrawn breath, cream did suit her, made a perfect foil for the spring flowers in her bouquet and in her hair...

On to the tiny church: a moment in the porch while Julie, small and blonde and perfect in her flowered dress, bent down to make final adjustments to the train before they walked down the aisle. Looking at it now, hearing the sounds of the little organ doing its best to sound resonant and majestic, she tried to recall how she had been feeling at that very moment, knew her heart had been fluttering in the strangest way as she saw the back of Finn's head. As she drew alongside he was caught turning towards her, and there they were, those expressions, her own as much as his, all tender and dreamy, as romantic as ever seen on the faces of a conventional pair.

Her eyes blurred over just then and she was only vaguely aware of the rest, the marquee in the garden, the crowd of guests, the speeches, flowers, all the familiar paraphernalia, until the tape came to an abrupt end. Finn got up then to switch on some additional lights. Jane was trying to pretend she wasn't mopping her eyes and even Tony looked a bit affected.

'Well.' Finn returned, sat on the arm of the sofa, draped an arm about her shoulders and pulled her close. 'That was wonderful, wasn't it, darling? The problem is, getting married is such an exciting business that you haven't time to notice everything that's going on, so at least the video solves something. I didn't realise my cousin was wearing such an ancient hat...'

'Oh, and did you see your Aunt Faye, Briony?' Tony broke in. 'Quite squiffy with all that champagne, although she always swears she can't touch alcohol. Even sherry trifle is a very chancy dish to offer her.'

'Anyway, it was a wonderful day.' Listening to Finn, Briony couldn't help being grateful. It would have been so easy for him to give her parents a hint that things were less than idyllic, but he was being so amiable, so charming and... 'You both did a superhuman job in such a short time, made it a day we shall always remember. Briony and I are truly grateful.'

'Yes, we are, Mum. And Dad.' Getting up, she kissed them both. 'Especially, as Finn says, when we gave you so little notice.'

'Well, it was something of a rush.' Her father spoke drily. 'But we weren't going to opt for a hole-and-corner——'

'Tony,' his wife interrupted firmly, 'maybe we ought to be going, darling. We have to be up early, don't forget, if you're going to cope with the church sale tomorrow. Anyway, if I can have the tape back, Finn, I want to have a copy made, then you can have the original. Something to show your children and grandchildren.'

'Jane.' The warning note in her father's voice struck Briony as odd, made her thoughtful as she

helped her mother on with her jacket as she stood
on the doorstep as they were going.

'Next time,' she could hear Finn suggesting,
'you must stay the night. It's a longish drive so
late.'

And her mother again. 'Thank you so much
for the presents. I'm going to love that Grasse
perfume, and Dad will enjoy the brandy.'

When Finn came upstairs after seeing them
through the gate, Briony was putting the last of
the dishes into the machine. She frowned as he
opened the kitchen door.

'Well, it seemed to go off all right.' Reaching
for a stick of celery, he crunched thoughtfully.

'Mmm.' She was abstracted. 'Thanks to you
and the couscous. Finn . . .'

'Yes?' About to disappear into the hall, he
paused.

'Was there something odd about my mother,
just before they left? Dad too, something about
the wedding but I can't quite put my finger on
it.'

'Since you mention it . . .' He came forward into
the room. 'I think perhaps they are trying to
decide . . . is she? Or isn't she?'

'What?'

'They're wondering if you're pregnant.'

'What? Why on earth . . . ?'

'Rushed wedding, my sweet. You know what
people always think.'

'No.' She felt blood rush to her head.
'Surely not.'

'It was just an idea that crossed my mind. Do you mean to tell me your mother never asked if there was any reason for the rush?'

'Yes.' Biting her lip she forced back tears. 'Yes, she did say something at the time but...I... Well it was so far-fetched it hardly registered and she didn't force the issue.' So delighted I was marrying you and not Edward, she thought but didn't say.

'Not that far-fetched.' The phrase seemed to have annoyed him. 'It's happening all the time, in case you hadn't noticed.'

'Yes, I know it is. But I certainly didn't expect my parents to think that I...that we...'

'Parents can be very suspicious people, especially where an only daughter is concerned.'

'Well, they needn't have been.' Embarrassment was causing her some irritation. 'Then, now, or in the foreseeable future. I'm not ready for that stage in my life. Not nearly ready.'

'No?' The ease of his manner was deceptive, of that she was well aware, especially when he moved so decisively to block her as she went from the kitchen across the hall in the direction of their bedroom. 'But yours is not the only opinion which is relevant, is it, Briony?'

'The only one I'm prepared to consider right now.' Dodging past, she strode into the bedroom, paced the floor a couple of times before sitting down at the dressing-table, picking up a hair brush and beginning to stroke with agitation.

'Well, maybe I'm not prepared to indulge you indefinitely.' Even his reflection was dominating, unyielding enough to cause a little *frisson* of nerviness.

'Huh,' she dismissed childishly.

'Do you remember once you asked me——' he spoke as if they had shared years of discussion instead of a few weeks '—why I married you?' Completely relaxed, he sat on the corner of his bed, pulled at his tie and began slowly to undo the buttons of his shirt. As she made no reply he raised one eyebrow and continued. 'It was quite a fraught moment, as I recall, and I'm not sure that the answer I gave was entirely satisfactory, but now I can explain more fully. I felt the need of a family to belong to. A wife and children, though by no means necessarily in that order, and you came along, a damsel in distress just at the right time. As someone said in a different context, I thought you were a perfect physical specimen and would probably produce some attractive children, plus of course the right kinds of grand-parent——'

'I think——' she swung round on her seat almost spitting out the words '—that's the most disgusting reason for anyone to get married.'

'Not as disgusting as marrying out of pique and spleen. Not nearly as disgusting as that.'

Those words she chose to ignore. 'Why didn't you get someone else? Someone from your own circle—Valentina Barossa, she would probably have jumped at the chance.'

'She might at that.' He pursed his lips as if in retrospective regret which she realised at once was only part of his game. 'But as you may know, Valentina has already had two husbands—that in itself is a pretty poor recommendation for number three. And I don't like coming third in anything, believe me.'

With such an ache in her chest Briony was half afraid to open her mouth, but she refused to allow him the last word. 'This conversation is becoming ridiculous.' Turning to the long wardrobe mirror, she reached behind for the zipper of her dress, unconsciously taking in the tumble of shining dark hair, the figure-hugging brown sheath as it slipped from her shoulders. When she had chosen it earlier she had wondered, half excited, if Finn would approve, if at the end of the evening he would...then as her dress fell to the floor she bent to pick it up, straightened and became transfixed as she saw how he was looking at her.

'Not ridiculous.' Smiling he took a step closer, turning her round, putting up a hand to comb fingers through her hair, pulling it back from her face. 'Not in the least ridiculous.' As his hand slipped down to her shoulder, a strap was brushed aside, exposing one breast. His head bent, mouth touching with bewildering brevity. Hit by a stomach-churning sensation, she gasped, closed her eyes for an instant then, about to raise both hands to press his head closer, she discovered that Finn had moved away in the direction of the bathroom. 'But when you're ready, let me know.' A moment later she heard the hiss of water as the shower was turned on. There was a stifled sob as she reached blindly under her pillow in search of her nightdress.

Such cruelty stunned her; it was difficult to accept what he had said and yet...so many things which had been difficult to reconcile were now becoming clearer. Unacceptable but...clearer. Only...it hurt so much.

Slipping the thin cotton over her shoulders, she pressed one hand to her breast, to the very spot where his mouth had burned a moment before. So that was all she meant to him, a prospective mother for his children, when all along she had imagined...that he liked her.

Well, he did of course, she had no reason to think he didn't—otherwise he would hardly have chosen her for what was so clearly an important role. But that no longer seemed enough...not nearly enough.

Sounds from the bathroom caused her to reach hastily for the light switch and she lay down, trying to control her breathing and feign sleep. A wife and children; the words, the tone of his voice echoed insistently in her brain—by no means necessarily in that order. That seemed the unkindest thing of all and she bit her knuckles quite fiercely to dam the sob that was threatening. Not nearly enough.

# CHAPTER SEVEN

'BRIONY!' The morning after her parents' visit, Finn's voice woke her, insisting she come back to life no matter how sleepy or reluctant...

'Wh...what?' Stretching an arm from beneath the duvet, Briony blinked and yawned. 'Oh, for goodness' sake, isn't it Saturday?' It was a wail of disbelief.

'It is Saturday. I'm sorry, I thought you must be awake by now. It's the telephone for you. Julie—she was most insistent...'

'Julie? Oh...' Another groan as she swung her feet out of bed, combing back her hair with one hand. 'I wonder what...' Padding barefoot into the hallway she picked up the receiver as Finn disappeared through the kitchen door. Was it her imagination or did his rear view indicate disapproval? Then her mind clicked; she remembered one reason why Julie might possibly want to speak to her and she was overwhelmed with guilt that she still hadn't spoken to him about the flat. She hoped, prayed that Julie hadn't. 'Hello?' Agitation made her sound all breathless.

'Hi, hope I didn't disturb anything.' She sounded revoltingly coy and knowing.

'No, of *course* not.' Finn crossed to the small room he used as his study without a glance in her direction. None of the exchange of tender glances you would look for in newly-weds, she thought with a tinge of self-pity.

'Sure?' Julie was being annoyingly persistent. 'Finn said you were asleep.'

'I was. He on the other hand has been up and about for some time.' Briony felt a touch of impatience; her feet were beginning to feel the chill of bare wood. 'Was it something very important, Julie?'

'About the flat, Briony. Nigel and I are off this weekend and wondered if we could pick up a key, have a look round, you know, try to plan things.'

'You haven't wasted any time, have you? You are sure what you're letting yourself in for, Julie?'

'Of course I'm sure. We both are. We want the flat and the good thing is, if we can move in at once, I can find someone to take over my present room, save a few weeks' rent on that. But I must let them know by Monday.'

'Yes, I see.' She was conscious that she was being hustled, had not originally meant to give Julie the go-ahead until she had spoken to Finn about it, but at the same time she didn't want to let Julie down. 'All right. If you want to call in you can have the key. I'll have it ready for you.'

'Bless you, Briony. See you in about half an hour, then.'

'All arranged?' As she replaced the receiver Finn strolled back towards the kitchen and shot the query towards her in a tone of total neutrality.

'What? Oh...yes.' Miserably she followed, watching as he set about topping up the coffee-pot, pushing some bread down in the toaster. 'Finn...'

'Yes?' He poured out two cups, pushed one across the table towards her and sat down, stirring, his whole demeanour uncompromising as he regarded her across the table.

'You remember we talked about my flat...about the chances of selling or...'

'Of course. You decided to sell.'

'Well, you see...the thing is...'

'Yes, I do see.' So cool and detached there was little room to doubt his blazing anger. 'That you changed your mind and instead decided to let it to Julie. And since I was not in your confidence, when she asked for the key I had no idea what she was talking about.'

'Oh?' Briony's spirits, already at a low ebb, slumped further. 'So she told you?' Against every indication she had hoped Julie might preserve some discretion on the matter of the flat.

'Yes, she told me she was going to rent—what you in short ought to have told me.' He took a slice of toast from the machine and began to spread butter in controlled fury. 'Said she and Nigel would like to have a quick look round before they finally moved in.'

'Well, you see...'

'Yes, I do see. I see that after saying you were going to sell your flat you changed your mind, decided to find a tenant, all without a word to me.'

'It wasn't quite like——'

'And I'm inclined to ask,' he interrupted as if she hadn't spoken, 'why this sudden change of plan, this decision to hang on to the flat after saying you wanted to sell?'

'It wasn't like that.' She spoke through gritted teeth, mainly because she recognised the truth of what he was saying. 'But really, you were the one who advocated selling. I was much less committed than——'

'Matters like that are usually joint decisions, wouldn't you agree?' His manner, the look in his eyes signalled contempt. 'And I'm still waiting to hear some explanation for your change of plans.'

'It's *my* flat, for heaven's sake, and there is no particular reason why I changed my plans.' Used to making her own decisions, she found it was intolerable now to have to consider someone else, and besides, his refusal to see any viewpoint but his own was maddening. 'Julie simply asked me if I would let her have my flat. *My* flat,' she emphasised. 'I've been paying the mortgage for five years, so surely I'm entitled to—— '

'*Your* flat, is it? And what would you say if I told you I was going to get rid of this place, put the whole property on the market lock, stock and barrel? My house?'

For a second she sat motionless, her heart missing a beat as she realised how much it had come to mean to her in the short time since their return from France, but then common sense reasserted itself. She relaxed. 'I wouldn't believe you—it means too much to you.'

'Mmm. Very perceptive.' He made it sound like an insult. 'But you are quite right. And in any case, I wouldn't make such an important decision without discussing it fully with you.'

'Well...I've no intention of getting into a slanging match,' she said righteously, and getting up she walked to the door. 'Besides, Julie and Nigel will be here shortly, so I'd better get some clothes——'

'That's right, when you're losing an argument, find some excuse to bail out.'

'I'm not losing.' With an effort she clung on to self-control. '*And* I'm not arguing. Only I *am* asking you, don't take out your irritation on Julie when she comes. She isn't responsible——'

'I am not likely to do that. Anyway, I don't give a damn about the flat—oh, I beg your pardon, your flat. I'm just surprised, that's all. Besides, I'll be in my den; I'm expecting a fax from Holland. It's likely I'll have to go off there for a few days next week.'

'Oh...' An unreasoning sense of hurt but still, an opportunity to get back at him. 'Oh, thank you for telling me.'

'Don't get on your high horse. I just heard of it a moment before Julie rang.'

She stared, knowing he was speaking the truth, but determined to give an impression of doubt.

'I'm sure.' She turned again towards the bedroom door just as his arm came down, a barrier of steel.

'You'd better be sure, Briony.' Judging by the straight line of his mouth, his feelings had by no means cooled. 'Don't make any more major decisions without consulting me, or at the very least *informing* me. Make me look a fool in front of your friends and you will regret it. And that *is* a promise.'

She ought to apologise; to anyone else she would have done so easily and without hesitation, but somehow with him... Knowing she was entirely in the wrong, the words felt as if they might stick in her throat. Nevertheless, she was opening her mouth to produce a few conciliatory words when he dropped his arm and, before she could voice them, the study door closed with a deliberation which was uncompromising. She was left with a sense of loss, of disappointment in herself which was hard to escape, impossible to rationalise.

It was a shock to find out how intensely she missed him when he went off to Venlo. The flat seemed cold and empty, lifeless and sterile. She was lonely, for heaven's sake, something she had never been in all the years she had been on her own. Then she had revelled in the feelings of privacy which her own front door had afforded. Occasionally she heard the students in the downstairs flat, and would pause as a muffled burst of laughter through the open windows seemed to increase her sense of isolation.

One night Finn rang from his hotel, telling her that the negotiations for the sale of several of his series to a number of European companies were going well. He threw in one or two comments about being tired and longing for home. And she, fool that she was, about to let him know she was missing him, was seized by a quite uncharacteristic shyness which held her back till it was too late. Someone came to his hotel door and he was forced to ring off. 'See you Thursday, Briony.'

As compensation, she planned to make the day a bit special, a welcome-home dinner which would set the scene for something of a reconciliation between them. After all, she told herself as she pored over cookbooks, they were married and must work to make it a success, and she completely discounted any more emotional ideas she might have on the subject. Her curry, she decided, might not reach the standard he was used to; something simple, salmon *en papillote*, was comparatively foolproof.

Thursday was inevitably busy, her day for private patients who came to the rooms she shared with a group of consultants and a psychotherapist. It was a convenient arrangement in that they could share one secretary who kept track of all their appointments, and the equipment was on the premises. It also offered a bit of scope for shopping as they were only fifty yards from a shopping precinct, and that day she found herself stimulated, even a bit excited, at the thought of welcoming her husband home from his odyssey with a delicious intimate dinner. Those pretty green table mats which had been a wedding present could have their first airing; she pondered over wines, added one or two names to her growing list and, after checking with Barbara, decided she could just about fit in a hairdo. She had not indulged herself since the wedding—critically she viewed her reflection. A trim and a nice bouncy blow-dry would do much for her morale. In her mind she was already wearing the bronze harem outfit which had had such a dramatic effect on the honeymoon. There was another top she might wear but... better to stick to the original. There was no telling if he would remember, but...

Laden but satisfied, she struggled back to the consulting-rooms, approved her hair as she hastily scrubbed her hands, and slipped into her short white coat. 'I'm on my way,' she mouthed to Barbara, who was on the phone apparently dealing with some complicated arrangements, and what her sudden stabbing gesture in the direction of the door meant, Briony could only guess but... She turned the handle and went inside.

'Briony.' The young man got to his feet with the aid of a stick, lips twisting in discomfort.

'Edward.' Colour washed into her face then as suddenly subsided, leaving her weak and shaken, though that might have had something to do with a missed lunch. Quickly she gathered herself together. 'Do sit down,' she invited, reaching her own seat just before her legs gave way, at the same time reaching for the case-notes which Barbara had placed on the desk, although in this instance they contained little information except for Edward's name and address and a line which said something about back pain.

'Now——' shaken as she was, she determined to act normally '—what brings you here?' Putting down her pen she leaned back, adopting her most sympathetic professional manner.

'You're looking wonderful, Briony. Stunning.'

'Oh . . .' Another blush. 'Thank you. Now, tell me, what exactly is the problem?'

'You, Briony.' He shrugged, a little shame-faced gesture which at one time she had found heart-melting but which now seemed very slightly contrived. 'You, Briony, are my problem. Always will be.' A little lopsided smile which was also familiar.

'Medically speaking.' Determined to be firm, she picked up the notes. In any event she was in no mood to examine the runes. 'So you hurt your back?' She got up and came round the desk, anxious to get on with whatever needed her attention. 'What happened?'

'I twisted it when I was playing squash. Now I can hardly walk.'

'What does your GP say?'

'Oh, I haven't been to him, all he'll give me is some pain-killers. No, I came straight to you first.

I knew no one else would do me any good.
Besides, I've been longing to——'

'If you could just take off your jacket... And
could you manage to get up on to the couch?'
Narrow-eyed she watched, surprised by her own
suspicions, but he did seem to be having a little
trouble with the right leg.

'I don't think——' after a quick examination
she indicated that he should sit up '—there's any
real damage, maybe a slight strain.'

'I've been hoping you might give me a
massage, help keep me going.'

'I'm not sure...'

'Please, Briony. For old times' sake.' He wasn't
put off by her cynically raised eyebrow. 'You see,
I've a whole series of business engagements, I
can't afford to cancel any...'

'Oh, all right.' It was probably the quickest way
of getting rid of him. 'If you'd just take your
shirt off....'

For some time she kneaded and manipulated,
astonished at her own detachment—impossible
not to compare Edward's white skin with that
other male torso she now knew so intimately.
'There.' Finishing with a sense of relief, she
turned and began to wash her hands, advising
over her shoulder, 'I'll give you a list of exercises
but be very gentle, and if you have any further
trouble I advise you to go to your doctor. Oh...'
She turned, drying her hands on a towel. 'You
might try losing a few pounds.'

'Ah.' Disconcerted, he stopped pushing his shirt inside the waistband, patted his stomach and grinned boyishly. 'Maybe I am gaining a bit, all those executive lunches.'

'Mmm, so how is the job going?'

'The job's all right.' He was looking at her with a soulful expression. 'It's my personal life that's shot to pieces.'

Turning away, Briony reached for her notes. 'Well, I think your back will soon be back to normal and——'

'I made a hell of a mistake, Briony.' Coming round the desk, he sat on one corner and put a hand under her chin so that she was forced to look at him. 'Pammy and I are totally mismatched. It was you and me from the start. Always was.' His manner was increasing in confidence. 'Always will be, eh, Briony?'

A series of images blotted out the present. She was reliving that first evening at Duncan Harraby's party, then Finn's flat, the wedding and the phone call from Edward which had successfully wrecked the day for her, but that—she caught her breath—that might have been his sole intention. The joys of Provence were on the periphery of her vision but she wouldn't embark... Not when Edward was... She heard her voice, cool, totally dispassionate. 'And what about...the baby?'

'Oh, I told you, didn't I? Pamela decided on an abortion.' His tone was the one he might have used to report an ingrown toenail, and she repressed a shiver.

His child and Pamela's—how could they be so heartless and unfeeling? If it had been hers, hers and Finn's, she would have felt as though the heart were being ripped from her body. Her eyes glazed over with pain and she came back only when he shook her slightly.

'Love, where did you go?' He smiled, then became serious. 'I know I've been all kinds of a fool, but you'll forgive me, I know. You always have, and some things don't change. You will, won't you?'

'What?' Abstractedly she looked up. 'Oh...yes, Edward. Of course I forgive you. In fact...'

'I *knew* you would.' He made no attempt to disguise his triumph. 'And now we can take up where we left off. I've got such plans for us...'

Something of what he was saying penetrated her thoughts. 'What...what do you mean, Edward?' She got up and walked round her desk but he got to his feet, rather nimbly she afterwards recalled, put out his arms and drew her into a crushing embrace.

'This,' he whispered against her cheek. 'And this,' sliding his hands lower. 'All the things that have been driving me mad for years and now——'

'But haven't you forgotten something, Edward?' With some difficulty she forced herself away. 'I'm married now. Married to Finn.'

'Yes.' His eyes darkened then he smiled. 'And it worked. I was driven mad with jealousy, thinking of you and Finn. But now, all things considered, it has turned out not so badly. You know what they say about forbidden fruit. We can meet any time you like and I promise, Briony, I'll never let you down again. It was just——' he dropped a forgiving little kiss on her forehead '—you were so strait-laced, my sweet, and I was so frustrated—that and nothing else drove me into Pamela's arms.'

'Really?' Her detachment, her calm, astonished her. 'So what you're saying is, if I had behaved differently——'

'I don't want you to change in any way; you're quite perfect as you are.' He spoke with blinding superficiality.

'But you were saying, more or less, that what happened was largely my fault.'

'Well...partly,' he said magnanimously. 'I don't want to avoid my share of the blame. Now tell me, darling, where can we meet? And soon, please.'

'Edward.' She felt as if she were dealing with a particularly aggravating child. 'You accused me of being strait-laced, so... why suddenly have I changed?'

'What?' He stared blankly, having no idea of how her mind was working.

'I am married now. And just as opposed to casual affairs as ever I was.'

'Casual?' His tone was deeply hurt. 'How can you say that, Briony, when we've been a pair since we first met? I'm talking about a lifelong commitment and I know you want me as much as I want you. I *know* that,' he insisted. 'You cannot mean what you're saying...'

'You're beginning to sound like a spoiled tennis player and——' a glance at her watch '—I have another patient due.' She reached for the door-handle. 'I'll see you around, Edward.'

'You can be sure of that.' A shade of bluster. 'I'll be back—I shan't be the one to throw away everything we had...'

A moment later he had gone and she was glad to sink down on to her chair for a moment, face buried in her hands as she tried to adjust to an entirely new concept. How...? When...? What had happened to make her fall out of love, totally and permanently out of love with Edward Spurling? She would never, not in a hundred years, have believed herself to be so fickle. And yet the feelings of relief were overwhelming.

That perhaps had a great deal to do with her reaction later, when the fruit salad had been carefully prepared, the salmon buttered and herbed, folded lovingly into those tricky little envelopes and placed on an oven tray, tiny new potatoes waiting to be steamed, green salad ready for its dressing.

And she herself, perfumed and powdered with even more attention to detail, the silks rubbing excitingly over bare skin, the high-heeled thonged bronze sandals drawing attention to pink-tipped toenails, could scarcely have been sending out stronger signals and . . . She paused by the mirror in the hall, smiled into the topaz eyes, ran the tip of her tongue over glossy bronze lips, turned to make a minute adjustment to the candles on the table which she would light in five minutes . . . And then the telephone shrilled, breaking into her idyll . . .

Her first reaction, one which she indulged, was to throw herself on to her bed for a storm of weeping. And then, angry with such weakness, she got up, hastily mopped her eyes and went into the kitchen to survey all her futile preparations. It was just a step from there to tip the salmon and the salad into the waste disposal, a gesture of foolish pique which she almost at once regretted. At least she might have taken it downstairs and offered it to Kate and Tansy who could have used it. She might even have asked them to come up and help her eat it all; there was more than enough for three and in her present mood some light-hearted female company would have been more than welcome.

Come to that—her mood grew morbid—I could easily have rung Edward. He would have needed no second invitation to come and join her, in fact it might have been the perfect way of getting back at him once and for all. That, or something very like it, had happened in an old film she had seen recently where the heroine had . . .

Oh—she shook her head in disgust—what on earth was she doing even considering such an idea? She had no intention of going near Edward again. Pamela was welcome to him. If nothing else, his visit to her consulting-rooms had cleared up any remaining doubts she might still have clung to. She saw him now for what he was; unreliable, weak, very nearly shiftless, all the things about which she had been so defensive in the past, the facets of his character which might be endearing in a very young man but which should show signs of change once the early twenties had been left behind. Arrested development: Finn had used the term to describe him and she had been angry and indignant, but now she was forced to admit that there was a great deal of truth in the accusation.

Finn had been right. He often was, but on this occasion she was angry with him. If he had been forced for some reason to wait a day longer in Holland, he might have realised and given her a little more warning. It was such an anticlimax, for heaven's sake, to be keyed up as she had been, then let down at the last minute. It was the kind of thing you would expect from Edward Spurling—nothing he did would surprise anyone—but from Finn . . .

Anyway, what was the use . . . ? She sat in front of the television watching the nine o'clock news, munching a cheese sandwich, drinking a cup of instant coffee. He wasn't coming back tonight and it would be at least twenty-four hours before she would see him. It might have been six months.

# CHAPTER EIGHT

THE moment she opened the front door after work the next evening she could sense his presence—hard to say why, since everything looked much the same as it had when she left. It was merely a feeling of life where it had been rather sterile. Then the door of their bedroom opened and he was standing here, dressed in a small towel, rubbing his head with another, beads of moisture still clinging to the hair of his chest and, like a blow to the stomach, she was back to those days in Provence when she had surreptitiously watched, had admired without realising there was as much longing in her emotions. Suddenly he looked up and saw her.

'Briony.' He came over, dripping some water, she couldn't help noticing, on the dull sheen of the wood. 'I didn't hear you come in.' Bending his head he touched her mouth with his, tasting of soap and toothpaste. 'What sort of day have you had? Busy?'

'Frantic.' His cleanliness was a reminder of how grubby, sweaty she felt. 'When did you get in? I must just get rid of these...' She indicated her clutch of plastic carrier bags and went into the kitchen.

'About an hour ago.' He followed her into the kitchen, and she was disconcerted by his intense scrutiny. Unnerved.

'And——' she reached into the fridge for a carton of milk, poured out a glass '—I'm dying of thirst. Tell me, how did your negotiations go?'

'Successful. Everyone tries to drive a hard bargain but in the end we got more or less what we wanted. At least, I think I can take you out for a meal this evening. To celebrate.'

'If that's what you want.' Somehow last night's anticlimax had left her drained; she had a feeling she might even be going down with the latest bug which was sweeping through the wards. She finished her milk, put down her glass and walked past him, shuddering as she was caught and pulled back against the taut strength of his body.

'I missed you.'

'Did you?' Her mood veered; his hands were tight about her ribcage, his mouth was nuzzling against her neck, causing the most irresistible ripples of sheer pleasure in the lower part of her stomach.

'I was surprised how much.'

'Ohh...' It came out as a sigh. No one had told her how wild and potent these emotions could be or, if they had, she quite simply had not believed them. Such sudden euphoria lifted her out of her depression and straight up into the stratosphere. 'I missed you too, Finn.'

'Did you?' Powerful arms whirled her round to face him. He seemed determined to etch her image on some internal camera. 'Truly?'

'Truly.' She tried to laugh, shook her head reprovingly, but his expression caused her to catch her breath. 'Truly.' A pause. 'Finn...'

'Mmm.' He sounded distracted, quite unlike his normal positive controlled self.

'I *must* go and wash,' she smiled, whispering. 'There's a strong whiff of antiseptic about me and I must try to get rid of it.' Firmly she detached herself.

'The water's hot.' He followed, stood watching as she moved about in the bedroom, hanging up her jacket, removing her watch and... Nervously she began to wonder just how long he intended...'I like your hair.' Absurd gratification that he had noticed. 'You've had it done.'

'Mmm.' Instantly reminded of yesterday's disappointment, 'Specially for you' she wanted to say, but why give him the satisfaction? 'Yesterday.' He ought to be able to work it out for himself.

'Pity!' Still he lounged in the doorway, watching every move, unnerving her. She kicked her feet out of her flat shoes, curling her toes into the pile of the carpet.

'Pity?' Surely she had misheard. 'What on earth do you mean? You just said you liked it.'

'I do like it. But I was simply planning...a long relaxing shower, and that would be devastating for your hair.' His eyes were dark and yet, with the light from the window striking on his face, tiny flashes of silver added something like an electrical charge which was undeniably exciting. 'A shower,' he continued, '*à deux*,' smiling as the wave of colour hit her cheeks. 'I seem to recall, it gave general satisfaction when it was tried before. I'm sure it would do a lot for both of us...'

'I...' In fact, what she had had in mind had been a long soak in a bath rich with restorative essences, but persuasive recollections flashed into her mind and she heard herself say, 'I could wear a shower cap.'

Smiling he came towards her. 'Not the same thing. Not the same thing at all.' His voice had that low mellow quality she had always found attractive, even before she had... 'I want to see you hold your face up, watch the droplets hang on your lashes, flatten down your hair till it's like a black cap. I want to see your toes, I want to soap your back...'

'No, Finn.' Smiling, she put up her hands to cover her head with complete insincerity—she had now abandoned any resistance to his suggestion. 'If you had any *idea* how much this costs at Hairlines...'

'Forget about the price. Didn't I tell you, I just signed a contract for any awful lot of money, so...'

'*And* you said you'd be back last night.' Thoughts of the salmon were still niggling.

'I'm sorry about that.' His fingers went to the buttons of her blouse. 'But then maybe I'm not. So...what's your answer, my sweet?' It was a totally rhetorical question, for she was smiling at him, her fingers tangling with his as they hurriedly began to deal with fastenings...

'Damn this bed.' She had been drowsing, drifting, halfway between heaven and earth when he stirred uncomfortably, adjusting his weight to his right side. 'What on earth are we *doing* here?' His mouth brushed her forehead. 'Why didn't I carry you into one of the other rooms after...'

'Impatience perhaps...' She raised a languid hand to caress his cheek.

'Single beds for a newly married pair—whoever would believe it? And all because you had decided to put me in my place—confess.'

Briony giggled. 'And of course, once you're put in your place you stay there. We can all see that.'

'Are you sorry?' A wisp of hair was brushed gently back from her forehead. He moved again, supporting himself on one elbow so that he looked down at her while she, obeying the demands of her own instincts, raised her hands, sliding the palms across the contours of his chest.

'Don't.' Her voice was less than steady when she spoke. 'Don't ask leading questions.'

'No?' He caught and held one of her hands as it hesitated. 'That...is very, very...' His smile, his faint frown explained when the words failed, and there was a shuddering groan which brought casual conversation to an end for a time and then ... 'Has anyone ever told you you have the most amazing eyes, all tawny and gold like a tiger's?'

'Well, funny you should ask that; a man I used to know, way back once ...'

'And——' he put his fingers over her mouth '—and those incredible sooty lashes.' A finger touched, delicately, experimentally. 'Just like silk. I brought you a present from Holland.'

'Oh, exciting.' Dreamily she smiled up at him. 'What is it?'

'Well, get up and dress and then I'll give it to you. And after that, unless you continue to act the siren, we'll go out and eat.'

'Oh,' she pouted. 'If you had come back last night as you promised ... I had prepared a super meal and we wouldn't have had to move from the flat.'

'Sorry. Sorry.' He held up both hands to demonstrate abject apology. 'It couldn't be helped, you must accept my word on that. I was probably more disappointed than you were. I've always hated being away from home, I thought you knew that.' Which seemed to her to imply less than she would have hoped. 'And now——' he gave a light slap on an exposed expanse of her skin '—get a move on or I might even change my mind about that present. And besides, I'm starving.'

'I wish you would tell me what it is.' Languorously she rose from the bed, stretched out a hand for a clean bra, clipped it into position, then stepped into panties, all the while conscious of him lying there watching through half-closed eyes. 'Perfume is my guess.'

'I'll tell you when you're ready and you needn't keep guessing because I'm not prepared to give you a clue, not even if you go down on your knees and beg.'

'That'll be the day.' She grinned mischievously and reached for her flowered satin robe. 'Anyway, if you're determined to be difficult, two can play at that game.' She slipped her arms inside and pulled tight the belt. 'If you think you're going to lie there while I provide the floorshow then you are very much mistaken...'

'Spoilsport.' He uncoiled and stood up, stretched. 'Sure I can't persuade you?'

'Quite, quite sure; besides, ugh——' she wrinkled her nose '—my hair's still damp. I'll have to go and use the drier. All that time wasted yesterday,' she grumbled, 'and the expense...'

'Not wasted.' He caught her as she passed, held her against him. 'I told you it looked good. And forget the expense,' he grinned. 'You're married to a rich man now, don't forget,' then he let her go as she wielded the hairdrier.

'What should I wear, Finn?' she shouted above the motor.

'A dress might be nice.'

'Oh.' She frowned, though there was no earthly reason why he should have mentioned the harem outfit.

She decided on a brief cotton jersey dress, thigh-length, showing long slender legs, figure-hugging, with wide straps and low neckline. For a moment she wondered if it was a bit too much, though the colours, black with white spots, were conservative enough, but his reaction when he appeared in pale linen trousers, a dark jacket slung over one shoulder, was reassuring.

'You look . . . good.' The warmth of his glance as it travelled from her face to her feet and back again seemed to suggest he was guilty of under-statement. 'And the hair looks as good as ever.' He came closer, cradled her against him, hands spreading down over her hips, hitching her closer. 'You deserve that present from Amsterdam,' he said huskily.

'Amsterdam?' An eyebrow arched. 'I didn't know you had Amsterdam on your itinerary.' Then she drew in a breath as he released her and produced a tiny box which could contain only one thing. 'A thousand pounds an ounce.' She made the joke to hide her emotions.

'Not perfume. Go on,' he encouraged. 'Open it.'

'Finn!' It was a gasp. 'Oh, Finn.' The icy glitter of precious stones took away her breath for a moment. 'Oh, I've never seen such a gorgeous ring.'

'Go on then, try it on, see if it fits.' And when she showed no sign of doing that he took the box from her hands, and an instant later the ring was sliding on above the wedding band. 'Looks right, don't you think?' And he moved her hand so that the small square emerald glittered in the light, the surrounding diamonds flashing brilliantly.

'I don't know what to say.' She extended her fingers, reluctant to look elsewhere for fear the ring would vanish. 'I've always loved emeralds but never expected to own one. They are so...opulent.'

'Well, it was a shame we were never properly engaged, but as I found myself so near Amsterdam it seemed the place to do something about buying you a ring.'

'Oh...' She was riddled with all kinds of guilt. 'And all the time I've been complaining about it. You went there specially to buy it?'

'Yes, so I hope I'm forgiven.'

'Totally.' Without thinking she stood on tiptoe, linking her arms about his neck. 'And completely.' For a long moment her lips, soft and inviting, rested on his.

'Well——' his voice was husky '—maybe we'd better go if we want to eat out...otherwise I can't guarantee we'll reach the front door.'

'Now...' They were sitting at a corner table sipping chilled white wine as they waited for the main course to be prepared. The little French restaurant where Finn was a regular customer was pleasantly full, though with tables set far enough apart to guarantee the diners an atmosphere of intimacy. 'You've heard all about Venlo and Amsterdam; now tell me what's been happening here since I've been away. Anything exciting happened; seen anyone?'

'Mmm.' Briony pursed her lips, at the same time lowering her eyes as she touched the stem of her glass. 'Nothing much.' The gems on her finger gleamed hypnotically. She would say nothing to spoil such a perfect evening; later she would tell him about Edward's visit, an abridged version of course. She would hate him to know about the suggestions Edward had made. 'Nothing at all unless you count Julie and Nigel. They've moved into the flat, and a party is planned for next weekend some time. I expect we shall be invited. Finn...'

'Yes?'

'I'm really sorry about letting the flat without talking it over with you. You were quite right to be angry.' Her hand reached out and touched his.

'No.' He smiled, enclosed her fingers protectively. 'I've thought about it a lot and I've decided I over-reacted. It was just...' He looked up as the waiter pushed a trolley close to their table. They watched as he deftly served the *canard au cassis* which they had ordered, refilled their glasses and then left.

'It was just...?' she encouraged as she picked up her fork and knife.

'Just...' He gave the impression of hesitation, perhaps he even changed his mind about what he was going to say. 'Just male chauvinist pride. Nothing else. To you, Briony.' He raised his glass.

'Finn.' The expression in his eyes made her feel absurdly shy and at the same time gloriously cosseted. 'To you. And thank you for such a perfect present.'

'In that case——' he smiled, touched his glass against hers '—to us.'

It seemed natural for them walking home to link hands, and there was no reason to say much except for an occasional appreciative 'Mmm,' referring to the perfection of the summer night, or maybe even of life in general. She was feeling delightfully dreamy, on the brink of acknowledging for the first time what had been lingering at the back of her mind since Provence. But soon they would be back in their own home, the door would close behind them and... they would be making love again and this time there would be no restraints, none of the silken bonds which had stopped her whispering, or even shouting, what she was feeling. This was the time to confess what she had been hiding even from herself: that she could no longer visualise life without him... And she wondered, with a tiny catch in her throat, if he too might be ready to make the declaration she so much longed to hear.

He had been right about her hair. As she sat at the dressing-table, hairbrush in hand, stroking idly, she could see it hadn't suffered unduly. It was as thick and shiny as ever. A little spray of perfume here, and here... The nightdress was the one she had worn in the hotel on that first night, the time they had fallen out so badly.

Would he remember it, she wondered . . . ? The door opened and he was standing there, looking at her.

'I . . . I feel I don't want to take my ring off.' Swinging round on the seat she smiled up, and was at once struck by the austerity of his expression.

'There's——' he ignored what she had said, and went on in a manner totally intimidating '—a message on the answering machine. For you.'

'For me?' She frowned doubtfully. The machine worked from his business number, one which none of her friends knew. 'You're sure?'

'Quite . . . quite sure.' A trace of sarcasm, perhaps even bitterness, then as she was about to leave the room, 'Here.' He picked up her robe and thrust it at her. 'Put this on, for heaven's sake.'

When she had finished in the study she found him in the sitting-room engrossed, or so it would seem, in a pile of typescript. He did not look up but asked in that detached way she found so freezing, 'You got the message?'

Deliberately she came forward but there was something nervous, uncertain, about the way she knotted the belt more securely about her waist. 'I know you're not reading that, Finn.' White teeth caught at her lower lip.

'No, you're quite right.' He tossed the pile of papers on to the floor, where they spilled heedlessly. 'I wasn't reading.' He got up, paced to the window and came back to stand looking at her.

'Well, I suppose you have something to say about this proposed meeting with my cousin?'

'It's all nonsense, Finn. Surely you don't imagine I would agree——'

'Just answer me one question,' he cut her short. 'Did you or did you not see Edward when I was away?'

'I did.' Her feelings were tearing her apart. 'But not in the way you think. Certainly not as he implied in that message.'

'You *saw* him.' Despair was in the way he raked fingers through his hair. 'And yet——' he was speaking through clenched teeth '—and yet when I asked you at dinner, you smiled at me across the table and denied that anything unusual had happened.'

'I didn't want to spoil our evening.' She stifled a sob.

'You didn't want to spoil... Well, you failed, didn't you? Conspicuously. But perhaps it wasn't so unusual.'

'Finn,' she said intensely, holding open both palms in additional appeal, 'it was my private clinic day, I——'

'Yes, I gathered that. He did go on about his reactions. Yours too. It was a massage——' that word was invested with the most indecent connotations '—you were providing, wasn't it? Tell me,' he invited scathingly, 'do you put postcards in corner shop windows advertising your services?'

She felt the blood leave her head, then reached out a hand to steady herself. 'How dare you ask me that?'

'First the flat, now this? Do you find it very difficult being honest with people? Tell me, did you have him here when I was away? Were you perhaps making love in my house? In my bed, even?'

'That is too contemptible to deserve a reply.' Then, since he made no attempt to reply and his expression was unrelenting, she clenched her hands in an attempt to retain control. 'Why for heaven's sake should I do that now? Tell me! All the time Edward and I were planning to marry he used every trick in the book to try to get me to sleep with him. If I wouldn't do it then, when I thought I loved him, why should I do it now when I know... It wouldn't make sense, would it?'

She broke off feeling it was useless, and for what seemed all eternity they stood there looking at each other, she waiting for an answer she felt sure would come in spite of his appearance of icy detachment. 'Oh, I don't know.' In contrast his tone was light, very nearly flippant. 'Some women develop an insatiable taste for it, especially after long periods of abstinence. I dare say you're one of them.' He walked to the door, pausing there with his hand on the knob but without looking round. 'I think I've still got a bit of jet lag to catch up with so I'll go to my old room for the time being. Goodnight.'

For a long time she stood without moving, then automatically walked round, switching off all the lights. After that there was nothing else to do but go into her solitary bedroom. And close the door.

# CHAPTER NINE

IT WAS the middle of the week before Briony felt she was at last emerging from shock, and Finn, she judged, was in a very similar situation. They had exchanged few words, she because she was feeling so desperately hurt, so misjudged that he could even begin to imagine that she and Edward... The very idea was enough to make her feel quite ill. And *that*, she recognised in a moment of rare amusement, said it all.

At breakfast one morning, Finn put aside his newspaper. 'You haven't forgotten have you, Briony, Friday is the awards ceremony.' Then in response to her blank expression he continued in a tone of patient forbearance, 'You remember, I told you it was on the twenty-fourth.'

'Oh...' She frowned; the mere thought of attending any sort of jamboree was distasteful in the present atmosphere of tension. She couldn't visualise it—going to a party, smiling, the sheer effort of making polite conversation, acting as a newly married young woman might be expected... 'Oh, do I *have* to?'

'Well——' he got up, went to the stove to refill his coffee-cup '—I don't suppose you *have* to.' Morosely he slumped back into his chair opposite, gazing across. 'There's no dire penalty for

154

not going. I don't know if it will make any difference if I say I *want* you to be there.' Her stormy
expression was one he was not prepared to
comment on at that time in the morning. 'On the
whole I suppose not.'

'If it's *so* important to you, then of course I
shall go.' Stiff with anger, cold with disapproval
as she was, she had no intention of handing him
an additional stick to beat her with,
although...since his opinion of her was so low,
she couldn't think why on earth she was
bothering. Pushing back her chair, she began to
collect dirty dishes, piling them into the machine. 'Are you working at home today or...?'

'No, I'm going to the studios. And I'll
probably be late, so don't wait supper for me.'

'All right.' She spoke briskly in spite of tears
stinging at her eyes. 'Don't wait supper' was beginning to sound like their song. But a moment
later she was able to produce a fairly rational
tone. 'When you finish breakfast, put everything
into the dishwasher and switch on, will you? I'm
going to have to rush.' A murmur from behind
the newspaper might have been anything, but as
she had no intention of repeating herself, she
settled for a hard glare before leaving the room
to pick up her jacket and bag, returning briefly
to say goodbye. 'Oh, and——' it was an after-
thought, not simply a reluctance to leave him.
'I forgot to ask, what sort of dress for the
awards ceremony?'

'Oh——' the paper was lowered '—something glamorous. Understatement at these affairs is to be avoided at all costs.'

'So you mean a long dress?'

'For the women at least.' A joke she supposed, as she hurried along the park in the direction of St Barnaby's, though neither of them had so much as smiled. And that more or less meant she'd have to try to find something this lunchtime; tomorrow there simply would not be time...

'What do you think about this, Julie? You don't think it's too...?'

'The only thing about it that's *too* is the price. If you can cope with that, then it's sensational. It will drive Finn completely out of his mind. I wish I had the kind of bosom to support an outfit like that...'

'What...oh?' Busily scribbling a cheque, Briony wasn't paying that much attention, then, 'What's wrong with your bosom?'

'Nothing that a few inches wouldn't go a long way towards curing.'

'Come on.' At the door of the boutique Briony paused. 'Since you gave up your lunch hour for me I'll treat you to a quiche and coffee across the road. You should——' suddenly she giggled '—you should have thought of that before, chosen Jack Tait instead of Nigel.' Dr Tait was one of the surgeons who had a lucrative private practice in cosmetic surgery. 'He would have been happy to make any alterations you required.'

'Yes, but what a price to pay.' They both giggled, and after they had given their order, Julie leaned forward confidentially, elbows on the table, chin supported by her hands. 'You and Finn are coming to our housewarming on Saturday, I hope.'

'Of course,' Briony said brightly. 'It'll be nice to see the old place again.' She smiled as the waitress put their order on the table.

'So long as you don't dress up to the nines.' Julie munched contentedly. 'It's strictly a jeans and shirt occasion. Oh, and you'll remember to bring a bottle with you?'

'I'll remember on both counts. But it does seem a shame not to make full use of the finery. I'm beginning to feel awfully guilty about the price.'

'Well, for the awards you have to have something to knock their eyes out—the competition is bound to be pretty formidable after all and of course Finn will want to show you off. I expect you'll be on TV. Don't forget, if you find a camera on you, wave madly.' They both laughed, then Briony sighed.

'You know, I've missed our lunchtimes together; there always seems to be so much shopping to do for two people, much more than twice what was needed before...'

'I'm finding that too. Why is it that the moment a man finds a partner he seems to opt out of all the domestic side of life?'

'Well . . .' Fair play compelled Briony to make a protest. 'Finn actually isn't too bad in that way; quite often he has the evening meal ready . . .'

'Huh. I'm beginning to wonder if Nigel simply wanted someone to iron his shirts. I'm sure he changes them much oftener now than he did before . . .'

'Oh, no, Julie, anyone can see he's besotted.'

'Well, that too. But I reckon that the shirts and food run a pretty close second.'

'Such cynicism in one so young and pretty. Well, much as I would like to sit here for the rest of the day, I suppose we ought to be getting back.' They went to the door before Briony said with a touch of diffidence, 'It is working out well for you and Nigel, Julie?'

'Yes, of course. Don't pay any attention to my moaning, it doesn't mean anything. It's just that I seem to feel so tired all the time.'

'Ah, well, I thought your doctor would have told you, you're missing out on too much sleep.' Briony grinned as her friend coloured up. 'What? Do you mean he hasn't advised you? Talk about professional negligence. Well, don't worry, it'll all sort itself out in time.'

Just as it has with you? she reproved herself cynically as she hurried along the hospital corridor. If she couldn't organise some sleep for herself pretty soon she was going to be in trouble, so what gave her the right to lecture Julie? It wasn't even as if her own situation owed anything to the demands of her husband . . .

*    *    *

'Well?' Holding her arms away from her sides she turned slowly, felt the swish of silk against her legs then paused, one foot forward, showing the knee-high slash in the black skirt, 'Well?' she asked again with a trace of anxiety. 'What do you think, is it all right?'

'Stunning.' He stood looking at her, little short of stunning himself, Briony noticed with a twist in her solar plexus, the detachment she was striving for gone in a second. The dark dinner-jacket and snowy shirt-front, gold studs gleaming on his wrists, might have been designed for such as Finn Lawrence, enhancing the width of shoulder, the lithe athletic figure. One hand slipped into his jacket pocket, the other flicked a few imaginary specks from the immaculate barathea. 'But then that's pretty normal for you.'

'What?' Having begun to turn, she swung back. 'What is?'

'Looking stunning. You must know that, Briony. Whether you're coming back from work at the end of a hectic day, going out to the super-market or like this, dressed up for a gala evening, most of the time you have a look of laid-back elegance and style. Come on, now, many men must have told you that.'

The glow engendered by his first words was abruptly dispelled by his last which angered her with their implications. 'I haven't known *so* many men. Certainly not on the terms you are suggesting.'

'And what terms are those?' He came a step closer, blatant mockery in the grey eyes. A hand came up, circling her slender neck, causing a *frisson* of excitement to race through her. No matter how humiliating to admit, he had merely to touch her in a certain way... 'Briony?'

'You were suggesting...' If only the blood were not racing through her veins...

'I was suggesting——' he released her quite suddenly '—only that you must have been attracting men since you left the schoolroom—so many opportunities among the medics at St Barnaby's—which makes it all the more remarkable that you should develop such a hang-up for Edward Spurling.'

'Do we *have* to listen to this old tune again?' She glared at the grandfather clock in the far corner of the hall. 'I told you, all my instincts are to give this ceremony a miss, I've little interest in mixing with the great and the good, so——'

'You're quite right, this is not the time.' All at once, she thought, he looked tired and dejected. 'And I swear I can hear the car turning into the gate right now. Anyway, I meant it when I said you looked stunning. I expect everyone will wonder what on earth you're doing with a man like me...'

Which was total patronising drivel, she fumed in the far corner of the hire car as it edged through the busy evening traffic. Quite insincere. There had never been a man more convinced of his own worth than Finn Lawrence and no one,

none of his important friends whom she was due
to meet, would think other than that he had
married an insignificant nobody... Only she
wasn't into the role of complete doormat; she
would hold her head high and refuse to be
intimidated.

And certainly their appearance was reassuring
as they scaled the wide staircase, walked across
the rich carpet between gilded cherubs towards
high mirrors at the far end—reassuring and in a
strange way exciting. Together they were quite
striking; she had noticed as much in the wedding
video and the present view was confirmation, all
down to fine feathers maybe...

Being tall herself, she needed a man like Finn;
everything about him was right, lean, even
slightly hawkish, bronzed and fit. Not just
handsome, though he undoubtedly was, but hard,
strong, reticent in a way, the kind of man others
admired. Tonight the lock of hair which fell so
persistently across his forehead had been tamed,
trimmed, and certainly he smelt delicious, as if
he had spent an hour or two in a man's estab-
lishment in one of the more exclusive arcades.

And she... A quick double-take had confirmed the identity she had initially doubted. She
smiled at her own whimsy, and the outfit... Well,
all her reservations about the cost had been misplaced—it was, quite simply, a knockout. The silk
wrap skirt was topped firstly by a camisole in
cream satin, so daring and revealing that she
could never have worn it without the sensational

jacket, its colour a cross between amber and lime, full-fitting, thigh-length and belted about her narrow waist. Never in all her life had she worn anything which suited her half as much; the colour might have been designed to enhance her eyes and... Swiftly she drew in a breath, determined not to allow herself to be carried away, but there was a hint of transparency to the jacket... Taken all round it could only be described as... alluring.

With the clothes so romantic, the make-up had to be restrained, just the bloomy look which suited her skin so well; soft lipstick emphasising the full mouth, maybe a little more daring with the eyes, burnished brown on the eyelids, lashes too touched with gold. Hair fairly simple, brushed back from her face, a hazy fringe softening and intriguing, wildly extravagant earrings and necklace from a market stall, which had cost next to nothing but which swayed and jangled each time she moved her head.

Mr and Mrs Finn Lawrence: the doorman boomed out their names as they turned into the glittering room and to Briony it seemed that a sea of faces turned enquiringly towards them, all curious about the woman who had captured the most eligible... Her fragile confidence began to crumble and she hesitated until Finn's fingers enclosed her wrist. 'Steady, now.' He smiled down at her as if he really cared, cameras flashed and whirred, which explained much, and they followed the waiter who threaded his way among all the round tables, stopping at one close to the front.

Sitting down provided comparative obscurity. A weight dropped from her shoulders, and she was even able to smile naturally as Finn introduced her to people involved with him in the programmes. It was a relief too that they weren't sitting together; he was placed halfway round to her right, close enough but not directly in front of her. And in spite of her expectations, most of the guests seemed reassuringly normal, not the patronising characters she had created in her mind. In fact Finn's producer was so friendly that she found herself explaining her trepidation, so graphically that soon they were both laughing.

'No, seriously?' With his amazing blue eyes, grey hair and quite sexy American accent, Jem Blackstone would have been perfectly suited to the front of the camera, she decided. 'But I imagine you think Finn is a pretty ordinary sort of guy...so why did you imagine the rest of us are from outer space?'

'Why should she think Finn is ordinary?' The woman on Briony's right leaned forward. 'She's been married just a few weeks, for God's sake. None of us realises how ordinary you all are until we've been married at least six months.'

'My wife, in case you didn't realise,' Jem introduced, 'is a complete cynic.'

'Just a realist.' They were so at ease with each other that it was clearly a light-hearted if well rehearsed routine. 'Anyway, I think as far as Finn Lawrence is concerned, maybe he'll last a year.'

The banter continued, and Briony found she was enjoying herself, stimulated by the sheer amiability of the people around her. Even the food was good. As she ate she found herself answering questions about her job—curiously they all seemed interested in something so ordinary—and there was even an invitation from one wag across the table to allow her to practise her craft on his back.

'You can't embarrass me with back jokes.' Aware of Finn's attention, his eyes on her face, she could not control the rush of heat in her skin. 'I promise you, I've heard every *double entendre* there is about backs——' Perhaps fortunately, she was interrupted just then by a loud electronic hum and the announcement that the presentations were now imminent.

That was when she began to realise how tired she felt; it had been fun just talking but now her eyes were beginning to glaze over, and if she joined in the applause as winners were announced, that was automatic.

At the same time Jem kept murmuring in her ear, something she gathered to do with Finn, but there was too much noise round about to be able to hear clearly. So she smiled, clapped, stifled a yawn, forced her mind away from the thought of bed, tried to remember and to be grateful that the weekend lay ahead, the opportunity to recover and then...something intruded... She realised that everyone at the table had fallen silent, faces were turned expectantly towards the platform, there was an air of rapt attention and suppressed excitement.

'And——' the lissom young actress smiled determinedly as she struggled with the envelope, '—and yes, for his series, *Last Bears in Europe*, the winner is... Finn Lawrence.'

'Finn?' Bewildered she looked at Jem, who with the others at the table was clapping enthusiastically. 'Is he... Was he one of the nominees?'

'You mean he didn't tell you? You mean you weren't listening to a word I've been saying?'

She shook her head, attention now concentrated on the tall figure on the platform, hearing the few words of appreciation before he was on his way back, interrupted several times by friends who were determined to add congratulations, then at the table, not sitting down as she expected, but circling, stopping behind her and bending, touching her cheek with his lips, murmuring something, dropping the trophy on the table in front of her like a prize. 'For you, my sweet.'

'Finn.' Glowing eyes followed him as he sat down again. 'Thank you.' Impulsively she put her fingertips to her mouth and blew him a kiss before reaching out for the crystal bowl and studying it.

'There you are, that's most likely why he didn't say—he wanted to surprise you.'

'Certainly he did that.' Dreamily she slid a finger across the engraved glass, noting the space left free for the winner's name to be added.

'Mmm. He's quite a man, your husband.'

'Brave as well as clever.' Chris leaned sideways, raised an eyebrow at Jem. 'You going to tell her how he saved your life?'

'Sssh.' Jem frowned, lowered his voice. 'You know he made me promise not to say...'

'Well, he didn't make *me* promise——' turning so that her face was screened and denying Finn any chance of guessing about their conversation '—so I can tell you. It was nearly two years ago, they were making the *Bear* series, and one weekend they went skiing—they're both mad keen on the sport—miles off the beaten track. Anyway, it started to snow heavily, Jem fell and hurt his ankle—quite a bad break as they found out when they got him to hospital. He couldn't move, and he tried to persuade Finn to go and try to bring help, but he refused. What he did instead, he picked him up—can you believe it?— he picked him up and skied all the way downhill, and they reached a village just as the light was going. It snowed for two days solid so...what chance would Jem have had if he had been left? Makes my blood run cold even to think of it...'

'Sounds a pretty desperate situation...' This sense of hot pride was ridiculous. It had all happened when her relations with Finn were cool to say the least. Ridiculous, but it would be easier to stop breathing than to damp down her swelling emotions. And to think... Finn Lawrence had chosen to marry her. She still didn't know why; all those reasons he had given were suddenly irrelevant and... He caught her eye, and at once her heart was hammering against the silk of her dress, she was feeling as trembly as a girl and he was disinclined to let her wrench her eyes away even if she wanted to, which... For heaven's sake, would this affair never end? Now all she wanted was to take up the trophy and leave; she wanted to be alone with her husband, wanted to say, to do all those things which until now she had been too afraid, embarrassed, too angry to admit and... too shy...

Even as the thoughts were flashing through her mind the formalities came to a close, the subdued rush for the exit indicating that she had not been alone in finding the proceedings rather lengthy, but nevertheless she had to hang about as one person after another demanded Finn's attention. For the first time she felt excluded by the professional chatter.

'Don't forget now——' Chris leaned over her '—you're to spend a weekend with us just as soon as it can be arranged. It's high time Barnaby got to know his godfather a little better.' At his wife's back, Jem mouthed the word 'Soon' before he turned and hurried her off.

So he was godfather to their son as well as everything else. It seemed she knew very little about the man she had married. Thoughts drifted as she turned the ring idly on her finger, pleased with the way it gleamed and glowed in the lights overhead, but her husband's name, spoken in a low sexy voice and in a tone of excited intimacy, made her raise her head.

'Finn, darling.' Valentina Barossa, who figured so frequently in gossip columns as to be instantly recognisable, was now completing the continental embrace. It was the kind of thing Briony had disliked when demonstrated by Kitt; now she hated it. 'I could not be more pleased and excited for you.'

'Thanks, Val. In spite of suspecting all these awards, I find I'm rather pleased myself.'

'You clever boy,' Valentina gushed. 'And not to give a hint all that time we were together in Venlo.'

Although they took a few minutes to register, the words seemed to echo round Briony's brain. She felt a sense of oppression, a weight bearing down on her chest making it difficult, almost impossible, to breathe. And then she realised what had been said; there was a pain behind her eyes which was very nearly blinding as she reacted to introductions...

'Val, this is my wife, Briony. Darling, Valentina Barossa, a friend from way back.'

It was automatic to stand, to smile, automatic to be polite, to find the right phrases, acceptable responses. Automatic to conceal the desolation which had so abruptly overwhelmed her, her strained, fixed smile a cover for the most tearing destructive jealousy.

'Yes, of course.' Finn, fingers on his wife's elbow as he began to lead her towards the door, was agreeing with his 'friend from way back' that they must all meet up again soon. 'We'll do that soon, I promise. No, definitely no more excuses.' Then as they relaxed in the back of the limousine he sighed with sheer weariness. 'Thank heaven.' And as she showed no response he glanced over. 'I suppose you found the whole affair un-bearably tedious.'

'No.' She raised herself from her lethargy, flicked her eyes over in his direction. 'No, sur-prisingly enough I quite enjoyed it. Right until the end, that is.'

'Oh?' He frowned. 'Well, I agree it's a pity it didn't finish half an hour earlier. But anyway, we'll be home in a few minutes and you can get some sleep. I must confess that's all I feel like.'

To her it sounded remarkably like a rebuff, a rejection of all those tender emotions she had been experiencing before his old friend appeared on the scene. Even thinking of them now caused embarrassment. 'I wonder——' voice and hands were shaky, tears were being controlled with dif-ficulty and there was the additional strain of keeping her voice low because of the driver '—you were always saying we ought to have a talk——' she bit her lip '—a serious dis-cussion...but somehow it never seems to happen...'

'Well, certainly I don't think tonight would be——'

'Oh, of course——' restrained hysteria '—keep putting it off and maybe all the problems will go away.'

'If you want to talk tonight——' his voice was clipped, entirely controlled, but she had little doubt that he was icily angry '—then that's what we shall do. Anyway, here we are.' They got out at the front door, thanked the driver, and she stood shivering on the doorstep as Finn put his key in the lock.

Afterwards Briony could never explain how it happened—perhaps it was down to nothing more complex than weariness, maybe misery was taking its toll, but somehow as Finn pushed back the door to let her pass something caught her hand. There was a moment's absolute terror as the crystal bowl began to slip, a desperate attempt to catch it was misplaced and made matters worse, the dish struck the stone with the force of a small explosion and dissolved into a hundred pieces.

The moment was frozen as they both stood looking down, she willing the whole episode to go into reverse, to be a ghastly nightmare, anything that would restore the shards into one perfect whole. But it remained relentlessly and permanently smashed.

'Well now——' when Finn spoke the eyes she raised to his face were liquid with misery and appeal, and entirely ineffective for his anger was icy and absolute '—I'm sure that made you feel a whole lot better.'

# CHAPTER TEN

'FINN.' She was standing beside the kettle, apprehensive, even a little afraid as she waited for it to boil, then looking round as he came into the kitchen with a newspaper package which tinkled ominously as he dropped it into the trash can. There was little chance of her pushing the incident to the back of her mind. 'Finn, I can't tell you how sorry I am...'

'I shouldn't let it worry you.' He had tossed off his jacket the moment they came upstairs, and his shirt sleeves were folded back showing the strong forearms sprinkled with dark hair. 'It isn't all that important.'

'Of course it's important.' Somehow his reasonableness was making her feel worse; she felt her hard-won control threaten to slip. 'Downstairs you said...implied at least that I deliberately...'

'If it was deliberate, I'm sure it was subconscious.'

'I'm saying——' her teeth were firmly pressed together now '—I would not have had it happen for the world, conscious or subconscious. I was so proud of you at tonight's ceremony; you deserved to win the trophy, I feel sick that I——'

'I said don't worry. I know where they buy these things, they don't cost the earth and I can easily order another if I feel I can't live without it. Are you making coffee?'

She ignored the query though her hand reached out automatically for the coffee-pot. 'I was so proud.' She was almost speaking to herself. 'Not just for the award, but Jem was telling me about his accident, the way you saved his——'

'Jem had no right.' For the first time he was showing real exasperation. 'He did promise he wouldn't make a meal of it.'

'Oh, not Jem.' Instantly aware of a betrayal of confidence, she tried to make amends. 'I'm sorry I said that, but it was Chris who told me. She said *she* hadn't been sworn to secrecy...'

'It's the same thing more or less, but of course women can never resist chattering. Did she also tell you——' sarcasm made his voice sound rather hard and unfeeling '—about my broken arm?'

'No.' Not understanding, she shook her head. 'No, she didn't tell me anything about that. But how——?'

'There was no broken arm,' he explained with insulting patience and weariness. 'What I'm saying is that these things tend to become exaggerated. What I did for Jem is no different from what he would have done for me or anyone else. There was nothing heroic or superhuman about it. Besides, what was I supposed to do, leave him to die in the snow?' The twist of sudden pain on his face reminded her how his parents had died in a very similar situation, and she felt a stab of anguish on his behalf.

'No,' she answered at last, speaking very quietly. 'I would never have thought of you going off and leaving him alone.'

'Well.' He shrugged, sighed deeply. 'I'm not going to discuss it right now...'

'Then——' she couldn't imagine why she had brought up the subject in the first place. This evening, in the midst of a stressful confrontation, was the last time to choose, so she reverted to the more immediate problem '—I would like to replace the crystal bowl, so please tell me, Finn, where I can buy another one.'

'I said forget it. Certainly I'm no more keen on that topic than the last, or anything else come to that.' He bit off the words as if he were having difficulty controlling his temper. 'But since you seem to have the bit between your teeth, I don't suppose anything I can say——'

'I just think it's silly to keep putting it off.' She hadn't realised how near to tears she was until she heard the quaver in her voice. 'Ever since we've been married we've been planning to talk about all the important things...'

'And you're right, of course, it's senseless to keep postponing things simply because I——'

'It was your suggestion in the first place after all.' She couldn't imagine why she should be forced into the position of defending herself. 'When we were in Provence.'

'Of course it was. But things have changed a lot since then, don't you agree?' Without waiting for her to reply, he went on, 'Then, maybe it had something to do with the sunshine, but it was so much easier to be optimistic about the future than now.'

'Do you think so?' Emotion made her voice sound thick.

'Yes, I do think so.' He sighed. 'It's all such a mess but I'm prepared to shoulder most of the blame. I know I took advantage of the situation, hustled you into marriage against your instincts and when you were in no state to make a major decision. I played on your sense of wounded pride, thinking I had… It was a highly emotional evening particularly for you and I acted on impulse when I suggested marriage…' As the import of his words filtered through, Briony felt her spirits hit rock bottom. Impulses were what people regretted, so… 'Anyway, there you are…' His grimace indicated pain rather than amusement. 'I've made a complete mess of our lives; now all I can do is try to salvage what can be salvaged, try to restore matters with as much dignity as I can. I promise you, whatever you want I'll go along with. I'll make it as easy for you as I can.' He sighed, so desperately that she was half inclined to cross the floor and put her arms comfortingly about him, but before she could he had moved to the door. 'Just give me a minute, will you? I want to scrub my hands then we'll meet in the sitting-room. No use making these earth shattering decisions in the kitchen, eh?'

When he had gone she stood there, looking blindly into space. If previously she had thought she knew something of misery then she had been entirely, monumentally wrong. This, what she was enduring now, was misery, anguish enough to bring an easing hand to her heart as she struggled to cope with the pain. Her entire body ached, throat, eyes, head, but the seat of the agony was behind the chest wall, sharp and excruciating as a knife-thrust.

The sound of the bathroom door forced her to move. She put some things on a tray, added the coffee-pot and followed Finn into the sitting-room. He moved a little when she went in so she wasn't entirely sure that he had been looking at his mother's portrait, then he turned, took the tray from her and placed it on the low table.

'I didn't bring anything to eat.' Even in the depths of her misery the banality of the comment struck her; with their entire future in the balance, her life's happiness at stake, she was dealing in inconsequentialities. 'But if you would like something . . .'

'No.' Frowning, he shook his head. 'Nothing. Coffee will be fine.' He sat opposite and took the steaming cup she held out.

'I thought——' hands supporting her own cup shook as she raised it to her mouth '—the meal was very good.'

'What? Oh...yes. But I presume you didn't insist on us talking simply to discuss the merits of the catering at the ceremony.'

'No.' His hardness brought the sting of tears back to her eyes. 'You know it had nothing to do with that.'

'Yes.' His voice was overwhelmingly weary. 'Of course I know. And as I said a moment ago, tell me what you want me to do. I shan't try to detain you if you decide you want to go. It was a kind of madness on my part, thinking we could be happy with Edward's shadow forever haunting you.'

'I still can't understand——' for a moment she disregarded his reference to Edward '—I can't imagine why you wanted to marry *me*. Even if you were, as you said, anxious to settle down, to have children...' A brief laugh, very close to mocking, caused her to stop, to look at him, wide-eyed and questioning.

'Did I really say that?'

She continued to stare without really understanding. 'Yes, that's what you said.' Then slowly, 'Are you saying something different now?'

'I'm saying——' he gave an impression of choosing his words with extreme caution '—it was a reason which at the time it seemed expedient to produce.'

'Oh?' There was something here which was hard to understand, her brain was muzzy, clear thinking difficult.

'Anyway——' his manner had grown perceptibly bleaker '—as far as one can judge it seems
as if Edward is no longer keen to marry Pamela,
or she him perhaps, but is still determined to
pursue you. And you are not exactly averse
to——'

'What makes you say that?' His conclusion was
so far from the truth that she was shocked out
of her contemplative state to something approaching indignation.

'I'm judging by the message he left on the machine; he seemed entirely confident that you and
he had reached an understanding. Certainly the
conclusion was that you had not rejected...'

'Finn, I told you what happened, or at least
as much as you would listen to. At the risk of
repeating myself, I went into my consulting-room
to find him already there. I had no idea until
then——'

'Mmm.' How could a mere murmur sound so
totally sceptical?

'That——' indignation made her voice rise a
little '—that is exactly what happened.' What
reason did he have to doubt her? What right did
he have, especially in view of what she had heard
about his relationship with Valentina Barossa?
'Anyway, do you think you have any right to
criticise when it seems your own behaviour is so
far from blameless?' If only she could remain as
cool and detached as he always seemed to be...

'I'm not entirely sure what you're getting at.'
He was watching her very closely.

'You *know* what I'm getting at.' Sheer passion made her eyes flash as she got up, took a few agitated steps towards the window, gazed out unseeing over rooftops and trees, then swung round to face him again, her chest rising and falling as she strove for calm. 'You must know.'

'I promise you, I don't know.' There was such a strange expression in his eyes as he stood there looking at her and he closed the few yards between them before she knew what was happening. 'I have no idea.' She felt his finger trail the length of her silk-clad backbone, causing a nervous shudder. 'So tell me,' he ordered in a compelling, seductive voice.

'You were with *her*.' Refusing to allow herself to weaken, she threw the words at him, following them with a childish sob. 'When you said...' Feverishly she bit her lower lip, looked down at the stone gleaming on her finger, tormented herself with the idea that the beautiful ring had most probably been bought simply to salve his conscience.

'*Her*?' Now his fingers moved more confidently, investigating each individual vertebra. 'Tell me who you mean, Briony?'

'Valentina. That's who.' Her voice was choked, and she was desperate for a hankie though she had none with her. She drew in a shuddering breath, held it, waiting, willing him to deny her accusation.

'Valentina?' His manner was casual, unconcerned; her spirits began to ease. 'You mean in Holland? Well, of course she was there.'

'Oh?' She sighed deeply. If only she could choke back her tears, if she could hide from him just how much his admission meant. 'Oh?'

'Tell me, why should you mind?'

'Why should I mind?' She pulled away then, frowning, shaking her head at the strangeness of the notion. 'Well, in that case, why should you mind about Edward?' The unfairness of his attitude was staggering; it exemplified the double standards which still said that what was unacceptable for women was OK for men. There was a long silence when she glared up at him, but even in her anger the temptation was there to lay her face against his chest, to allow the easing tears to flow, to feel his hands stroking and comforting her...

'I should mind because of the relationship which exists—I had hoped that was past tense but apparently not—between you and Edward. There never was, nor ever will be, anything of the sort between Valentina and me. I thought I had told you that before.'

He had. Of course he had. She had been doubtful of his assurance then and was still more doubtful now. Anyway, he would say that, wouldn't he? And looking at her with that...that expression wasn't going to soften her in any way. 'Oh, yes?' A tiny scoffing laugh. 'So what was

she doing there? I don't imagine it was for the
skiing.'

The flicker of a smile drifted across his face.
'No, not for that. She was there in her capacity
as vice-chairman of the Spanish television
company she inherited from her first husband. I
thought you might have known about that from
some of the recent news reports.'

'I don't have time to read the gossip column,'
she said unctuously, at the same time determined
not to be tricked by any too easy assertion.

'You should perhaps make time . . .'

'Anyway, she looks as if she would like to eat
you.'

Now his smile was unrestrained, a genuine
smile, white teeth gleaming, eyes flashing, the
first real smile she had seen in days. 'I think if
she tried she would find me indigestible.' His easy
warmth was causing tiny ripples in her stomach.
'But tell me, if you had been right in all your
assumptions, would it have mattered to you all
that much?'

'Of *course* it would.' The words burst out
passionately, then, afraid of showing too much
of her deepest feelings, she repeated with more
restraint, 'Of course it would. No woman would
like to think of her husband having an affair with
someone else. Even if . . .' She broke off, gnawing
at her lower lip.

'Mmm. Even if . . . ?' He prompted.

'Even if he has married her solely as a suitable
mother for the child he would have liked to have.'

Throwing the words at him in that way showed how much suffering they had caused.

'So... even then, she might be... not jealous exactly, but——'

'Jealous!' In a second her frail hold on restraint was lost; there was a sense of relief as it finally slipped away from her. 'Yes, there's no need to shy away from the word. Jealous is as good as any since it describes so exactly how I feel.'

'Is that...?' His hands came up, drew her closer to him, and she stood, not resisting when he loosened the belt of her gorgeous jacket but knowing that the rapid rise and fall of her breast must be a clear enough indication of her feeling. And she drew in a swift breath as his fingers slipped beneath the thin silk of her camisole, moving with stealth over the warm skin, counting each rib and... aaah. It was an upward spiral of pleasure, intensified by the expression in his eyes, by the persuasive brushing of fingertips against the most sensitive areas of her body. And when he spoke she felt the brush of his lips against her cheek. 'Is that what you are saying, Briony?'

'That I was jealous?' Her head arched back, blatantly seductive. There was a certain madness in the course she was taking, she knew that, and for a split-second her resolve wavered, but then... she wanted this man more than she had ever wanted anything in this life before, and now the crisis point had been reached she knew she was going to fight to keep him. 'Yes, Finn, that is what I'm saying—that I was wildly, passionately jealous when I thought you might be having an affair with Valentina.'

He gathered her to him then, so close she felt the entire length of his body against hers, so close that his shuddering sigh might have been her own, so close she felt his tensions ease away with her own. Something touched the top of her head, light and feathery like the gentlest of kisses. She raised her face to look at him, oblivious of the tears wetting her cheeks.

'And I was going to say——' her voice was shaky and laughing '—to say, oh, so many things... I planned them at the ceremony. I had made up my mind, you see ... I was so proud... Maybe I had no right, but still, I was, and then...' She bit her lip. 'Then I heard Valentina say what she did.' Tears were still very close. 'And...I go and spoil everything by dropping the bowl...'

'Forget the bowl. I don't care about it. What I want to hear from you——' he put a finger beneath her chin, holding her face up to his, brushing a thumb over her lips '—is what you feel for Edward. Now. At this moment. If you were free, and he wanted to marry you, what——'

'About Edward——' her smile was slightly rueful '—I don't feel anything very much. I wouldn't have him out of pride even if I still loved him...'

'Even if.... Does that mean...?'

'Finn.' Impossible now to keep the smile from her face; all the tensions were easing away so miraculously, being replaced by the most wonderfully soft, tender sensations. 'I realised some time ago that I had never loved Edward. I can't explain what it was—playing at love perhaps. Once you told me that if I loved him, truly loved him, I'd have had to hang on to my virtue by the skin of my teeth, instead of which it was easy. No problem.' Gazing up into his face, the wide amber eyes gleaming, she was aware of a suffusion of warmth. 'Instead of which——' she raised both hands to touch his cheeks '—when the time came, I could hardly wait to give it away.'

His mouth touched hers so that for a long delirious moment she was aware of nothing but the intense pleasure of the contact, the persuasive pressure, then the parting of lips, the sensuous exploration, even the faint moan when they drew apart. Then lying with her cheek against his chest, her hands exploring the contours of his body under smooth cotton. 'What fools,' was his breathed comment against her hair. 'What fools to waste so much precious time playing games. Love games.'

'But think——' reaching out both arms she circled his body '—now we have all the time in the world ahead of us. But tell me, Finn——' the amber eyes searched his face '—you still haven't told me why you married me.'

'Don't you know?'

'Only what you told me.'

'That, my darling——' tender hands were smoothing hair back from her forehead '—that was not quite the truth.'

'Not *quite*?' A tiny frown. 'What . . . ?'

'The real reason, one I suspect you must have guessed, since I've given myself away so often, is that I've been mad about you since very nearly the first time we met.'

'Have you?' Eyes widened in surprise, in startled delight. 'But in that case——' she frowned as she tried to work it out '—why didn't you make a move?'

'If you remember, I did just that. I asked you to come with me to a film première, I thought you would be impressed, instead of which you shot me down in flames.'

'Oh, it wasn't quite like that.' But it was difficult to forget how dismissive she had been on that occasion—remembering brought colour to her cheeks.

'It was. *Quite* like that, and you know it. Damaged my ego beyond repair.'

She giggled. 'Yeah, I noticed. Well, I'd have thought if you were so mad about me you'd have shown more staying power.'

'Well, you see, I had a wager with myself that if you refused my invitation with any obvious regret I'd try again. If you rejected it out of hand which you did, then I'd put you out of my mind, forget you completely.'

'And that's why,' she teased with a hint of smugness, 'the next time we met you asked me to marry you?'

'I found it easier to talk about forgetting you than to do it. So on that night when we all found ourselves back here, you looking so distraught, I simply took advantage of the situation. I didn't plan it, it was an impulse. That was the truth but I didn't regret it. Not even when you cast me out of your bed on the night of our wedding.'

'Oh, I didn't.' The protest was automatic, then with a change of tack, 'I wonder if Edward deliberately chose his moment so he could mess things up between us. I've asked myself pretty much the same question ever since that message on the phone the other day. He was bound to have known you were the one most likely to use the machine. I'm beginning to think he was out to make as much trouble as he possibly could— the day of the wedding as well.'

'Sounds rather typical. To be fair to him, I think it was always you, Pamela was simply an accident.'

'Have you never liked him?'

'I don't dislike him. I suppose, after I met you, my main reaction to him was one of jealousy. Apart from that——' he shrugged '—you know his father cheated me. When my parents were killed he manipulated things so he had control of the company.'

'Oh, Finn.'

'Yes, Sir Julian, only he hadn't got his title at that time, managed to grab most of the assets while my share consisted of the debts. He's a pretty sharp operator and all these years he's been able to indulge himself: yachts, fast cars, women, all the usual "road to ruin" interests. But anyway, I understand it's all coming to an end; the bailiffs are waiting in the wings, to say nothing of the VAT men.'

'Oh... Poor Lady Spurling.'

'Yes, poor thing. I suspect she's the one who will suffer most. Anyway, that was another reason why I ought to have been able to forget you. If you were so much in love with cousin Edward—this is how my argument went—then you and I couldn't possibly have anything in common. I didn't even like the idea that we might have.'

'But——' gently she traced the outline of his mouth with a slender finger '—I'm hoping you might have changed your mind since then.'

'You could say that. Except that I was never able to convince myself in the first place. I loved you so madly, illogically, and could never talk myself out of it... only...'

'Say that again, Finn. Say it slowly. I want to make sure I'm not dreaming. You know, you've never said it before, not even when...'

'Ah, *then*,' he smiled. 'Then it was a great effort to stop myself, to keep from shouting it out at the top of my voice, only I felt so insecure...'

'Insecure?' Incredulity was in her voice as well as in her expression. 'Finn Lawrence, insecure? I find that hard to believe...'

'Nevertheless... Can you imagine what it did to me when you said you were hanging on to the flat after all?'

'Why?' she frowned. 'Why on earth should that make any difference?'

'To me it did. To me it suggested you might be keeping your options open so you would have somewhere to go if you decided you couldn't go on...'

'Oh...' Looking at it now she could understand how he might have got that impression. 'But I never would. I never thought...'

'Anyway, it doesn't seem to matter so much now.' Smiling, he was looking at her mouth.

'Say it.' Gently she put a finger to his mouth as she reminded him. 'Say it again, Finn, just so I know there's no mistake...'

'I love you, Briony, and I know I'm going to go on loving you for the rest of my life.'

Leaning forward she placed her lips against his, neither of them moving. 'I love you too, Finn.' Her voice was shaky, but this time with joy. 'So much that it hurts. I love you in a way I never believed possible, so much that I...' All at once she was overcome with shyness. 'I want to give you everything you want, to help fulfil your dreams. You remember that reason you gave me for marrying? Then if that is what you really want...'

'I can see——' his voice was tender, gentle
'—those words are going to be held against me
for evermore.'

'I want to show you...' The beautiful eyes had
a melting translucence which made him hold his
breath.

'You would do that, just for me?'

'If it would make you happy. I want that so
much and if that is what it takes...'

'Well.' He kissed the tip of her nose. 'I thought
I had explained to you that it was a mere excuse,
the only thing I could think of at the time since
the truth itself would have been inappropriate.
But can I confess that, right at this moment, the
subject is not really at the forefront of my mind?
Though I'm sure it will be eventually. For both
of us, I imagine.' The silvery eyes were gleaming
with amusement. 'I think perhaps we should
consider your mother; she seems much too young
to be a grandmother just yet, and besides...there is the matter of the sudden wedding
to be clarified. I think for everyone's sake it
would be best if all lingering doubts could be
removed...'

'Oh?' Her face was slightly pink. 'I'd forgotten about that.'

'Only...' Unexpectedly he swung her up in his
arms, walked to the doorway and across the hall,
not this time to the room they had shared but to
another with a particularly wide and inviting
double bed. 'Only,' he repeated, and she was uncertain if his breathlessness was caused by her

weight or some other factor, 'there is nothing in the world to stop us practising every love game we can think of...'

'Nothing,' she agreed, linking her hands about his neck and pulling his face close to hers. 'And don't they say practice makes perfect?'

'You're telling me——' his tone was incredulous '—it can get better?' And her lips opened beneath his as they shared laughter and delight.

ANNOUNCING THE

# FLYAWAY VACATION SWEEPSTAKES!

This month's destination:

## Beautiful SAN FRANCISCO!

This month, as a special surprise, we're offering an exciting FREE VACATION!

Think how much fun it would be to visit San Francisco "on us"! You could ride cable cars, visit Chinatown, see the Golden Gate Bridge and dine in some of the finest restaurants in America!

The facing page contains two Entry Coupons (as does every book you received this shipment). Complete and return *all* the entry coupons; **the more times you enter, the better your chances of winning!**

Then keep your fingers crossed, because you'll find out by June 15, 1995 if you're the winner! If you are, here's what you'll get:

- Round-trip airfare for two to beautiful San Francisco!
- 4 days/3 nights at a first-class hotel!
- $500.00 pocket money for meals and sightseeing!

Remember: The more times you enter, the better your chances of winning!*

*NO PURCHASE OR OBLIGATION TO CONTINUE BEING A SUBSCRIBER NECESSARY TO ENTER. SEE REVERSE SIDE OR ANY ENTRY COUPON FOR ALTERNATIVE MEANS OF ENTRY.

VSF KAL

# FLYAWAY VACATION
## SWEEPSTAKES
## OFFICIAL ENTRY COUPON

This entry must be received by: MAY 30, 1995
This month's winner will be notified by: JUNE 15, 1995
Trip must be taken between: JULY 30, 1995-JULY 30, 1996

**YES,** I want to win the San Francisco vacation for two. I understand the prize includes round-trip airfare, first-class hotel and $500.00 spending money. Please let me know if I'm the winner!

Name_____

Address _____ Apt. _____

City                    State/Prov.                    Zip/Postal Code

Account #_____

Return entry with invoice in reply envelope.

© 1995 HARLEQUIN ENTERPRISES LTD.                    CSF KAL

---

# FLYAWAY VACATION
## SWEEPSTAKES
## OFFICIAL ENTRY COUPON

This entry must be received by: MAY 30, 1995
This month's winner will be notified by: JUNE 15, 1995
Trip must be taken between: JULY 30, 1995-JULY 30, 1996

**YES,** I want to win the San Francisco vacation for two. I understand the prize includes round-trip airfare, first-class hotel and $500.00 spending money. Please let me know if I'm the winner!

Name_____

Address _____ Apt. _____

City                    State/Prov.                    Zip/Postal Code

Account #_____

Return entry with invoice in reply envelope.

© 1995 HARLEQUIN ENTERPRISES LTD.                    CSF KAL

# OFFICIAL RULES

## FLYAWAY VACATION SWEEPSTAKES 3449

### NO PURCHASE OR OBLIGATION NECESSARY

Three Harlequin Reader Service 1995 shipments will contain respectively, coupons for entry into three different prize drawings, one for a trip for two to San Francisco, another for a trip for two to Las Vegas and the third for a trip for two to Orlando, Florida. To enter any drawing using an Entry Coupon, simply complete and mail according to directions.

There is no obligation to continue using the Reader Service to enter and be eligible for any prize drawing. You may also enter any drawing by hand printing the words "Flyaway Vacation," your name and address on a 3"x5" card and the destination of the prize you wish that entry to be considered for (i.e., San Francisco trip, Las Vegas trip or Orlando trip). Send your 3"x5" entries via first-class mail (limit: one entry per envelope) to: Flyaway Vacation Sweepstakes 3449, c/o Prize Destination you wish that entry to be considered for, P.O. Box 1315, Buffalo, NY 14269-1315, USA or P.O. Box 610, Fort Erie, Ontario L2A 5X3, Canada.

To be eligible for the San Francisco trip, entries must be received by 5/30/95; for the Las Vegas trip, 7/30/95; and for the Orlando trip, 9/30/95.

Winners will be determined in random drawings conducted under the supervision of D.L. Blair, Inc., an independent judging organization whose decisions are final, from among all eligible entries received for that drawing. San Francisco trip prize includes round-trip airfare for two, 4-day/3-night weekend accommodations at a first-class hotel, and $500 in cash (trip must be taken between 7/30/95—7/30/96, approximate prize value—$3,500); Las Vegas trip includes round-trip airfare for two, 4-day/3-night weekend accommodations at a first-class hotel, and $500 in cash (trip must be taken between 9/30/95—9/30/96, approximate prize value—$3,500); Orlando trip includes round-trip airfare for two, 4-day/3-night weekend accommodations at a first-class hotel, and $500 in cash (trip must be taken between 11/30/95—11/30/96, approximate prize value—$3,500). All travelers must sign and return a Release of Liability prior to travel. Hotel accommodations and flights are subject to accommodation and schedule availability. Sweepstakes open to residents of the U.S. (except Puerto Rico) and Canada, 18 years of age or older. Employees and immediate family members of Harlequin Enterprises, Ltd., D.L. Blair, Inc., their affiliates, subsidiaries and all other agencies, entities and persons connected with the use, marketing or conduct of this sweepstakes are not eligible. Odds of winning a prize are dependent upon the number of eligible entries received for that drawing. Prize drawing and winner notification for each drawing will occur no later than 15 days after deadline for entry eligibility for that drawing. Limit: one prize to an individual, family or organization. All applicable laws and regulations apply. Sweepstakes offer void wherever prohibited by law. Any litigation within the province of Quebec respecting the conduct and awarding of the prizes in this sweepstakes must be submitted to the Regies des loteries et Courses du Quebec. In order to win a prize, residents of Canada will be required to correctly answer a time-limited arithmetical skill-testing question. Value of prizes are in U.S. currency.

Winners will be obligated to sign and return an Affidavit of Eligibility within 30 days of notification. In the event of noncompliance within this time period, prize may not be awarded. If any prize or prize notification is returned as undeliverable, that prize will not be awarded. By acceptance of a prize, winner consents to use of his/her name, photograph or other likeness for purposes of advertising, trade and promotion on behalf of Harlequin Enterprises, Ltd., without further compensation, unless prohibited by law.

For the names of prizewinners (available after 12/31/95), send a self-addressed, stamped envelope to: Flyaway Vacation Sweepstakes 3449 Winners, P.O. Box 4200, Blair, NE 68009.

RVC KAL